Titles available in the
SILVER THIEVES
series
(in reading order)

I0616577

Book 2

A CROOK'S TREASURE

A.E. STEWART

A CROOK'S TREASURE

Published by A.E. Stewart

Cover artwork by Gary Taaffe, Copyright © A.E. Stewart 2016
Formatting by Gary Taaffe, Copyright © A.E. Stewart 2016

ISBN: 978-0-9946151-1-4

Gary Taaffe
BunyaPublishing.com
BunyaPublishing@gmail.com

BUNYA PUBLISHING.com

PART ONE

— CHAPTER ONE —

A Legacy

England and Australia 1953

Jill left London with great regret because she had not accepted David's invitation to attend her Mum's wedding. After the funeral John and Myra had taken her aside and given her all the details regarding the deaths of Vanessa and David. It all seemed so bizarre. David Collins had been murdered for a spoon. Apparently it was a priceless relic which would be used as part of the Crowning Ceremony at the Queen's Coronation. How ironic that he possessed something which was stolen from the Tower of London and that he felt no guilt about keeping it. Her Mother probably died without knowing anything about it. Her mind flashed with the recollection of the other spoon which Myra found in Nan's kitchen drawer. David had shown some interest and encouraged Myra to investigate its history. She wondered how Myra would feel about it now.

When her plane landed Brian was there with their two children: their four year old daughter Frances and their two year old son Matthew. Jill couldn't help but notice that the children had grown taller. The tears filled her eyes as she realised that Mum would never get to watch these two grow up. It seemed uncanny that Frances already looked more like her dead grandmother than her own mother. Brian was so happy to have her home. The other words would come later, but that night, Jill clung to him as if she had been separated for months, not weeks.

'It was such a senseless killing, all over a stupid spoon. I can't understand why it was necessary to kill them for it. Myra told me that the spoon was locked away in David's flat with an incredible security system. Perhaps the killers wanted to get them out of the way first.'

'I understand your grief and also the devastating shock that you both have received, but nothing we can say or do will bring them back. What about Myra? What is she going to do now?'

'She said that she will stay in London for a while to wind up the affairs of the estate, but I have a feeling about those two. I don't think that she will be returning for a while.'

'That seems fine. She has been a single girl for some time. Perhaps a cold blooded Englishman may melt her heart.'

Jill smiled for a few seconds before replying.

'Don't you mean a hot blooded Englishman? John is English but he has lived and worked in South Africa for some time, but I think that he will return there after this is all over.'

'What about the Coronation? It is due to take place soon. Perhaps they will stay for that?

'Who knows? We'll find out soon enough. Meantime I'm so glad to be home. Just hold me,' said Jill as she snuggled closer to her husband.

'Everything is going to be o.k. Brian whispered.

England

David's will was read. Apart from the collection of silver spoons, he left nothing else to his son John. To Vanessa his wife, he left the Mayfair flat which was a valuable piece of real estate, but unfortunately Vanessa had no time to make a current will before she was killed.

When the Australian will was read, Vanessa had bequeathed her house to both her daughters. Although John was very understanding about his Father's will, somewhere something niggled in his subconscious. Why did his Father leave him with such a small proportion of the estate? He must have known that John would not want to keep the Coronation Spoon, so what was at the back of his mind?

'Dad wanted your Mother to have this house. And even though she didn't leave it to you and your sister in her will, you have every right to expect to inherit her estate,' John told Myra.

'But I already own half a house in Australia. With the proceeds of that sale I will be able to purchase something smaller, so I am more content with that arrangement. Apart from your inheritance of that priceless spoon, I believe that your Father left you very little.'

'Yes that is true, but don't forget that because of my position in the Cape Town Museum, I earn a very good wage and I own my own flat there.

I expect that the Coronation Spoon was a test of my integrity, but I believe that he knew that I would do exactly what I have done.'

'That is a noble attitude for you to adopt, but we can discuss this situation with your Dad's solicitor when you have made an appointment. The spring weather is so lovely, why don't I pack a picnic and we can enjoy the fresh air of Hyde Park?'

'Done,' agreed John.

All thoughts about the present concerns were forgotten by Myra as she basked in the gentle sunshine. She focused on John sitting next to her, slowly concentrating her thoughts on him. He was a special man. John looked at this lovely young woman who held his positive attention but perhaps his Father's will had become an obstacle between them. Today she looked so radiant. He almost reached out for her hand. Would she see something in this that was self-serving and not a genuine attraction which he knew he felt? This was not an easy path to tread. He had better take it slowly and give it some more thought.

'How much longer will you stay in England? The Coronation is fast approaching and I intend to stay and see it. What about you? Do you have any reason to go home just yet?'

Myra considered this half hearted invitation, but to give John his due, she knew that they both had some legal work to address, and she did want to see the Coronation. After all she was responsible for returning the Coronation Spoon.

'In answer to your question, I'm not in any hurry to return to Australia. This is a once in a lifetime event, so I will stay for it too.'

John nodded in agreement but he knew deep in his heart that although Myra and he were bound by destiny in many ways, this situation needed careful consideration.

CHAPTER TWO

John Plays it Cool

An appointment was made with the family solicitor. John said very little except that he accepted his Father's wishes regarding the Mayfair flat passing to Myra's mother as bequeathed. Myra expressed her own thoughts about this. After a minute the solicitor said.

'Myra and John, I have to tell you that in my profession one sees many strange bequests. I understand that although Myra has admitted to owning a half share in her late Mother's home in Australia, she does not totally agree that this Mayfair flat should be passed only to herself and her sister. This is because her Mother did not leave it to her in her current will.'

John repeated. 'I have no intention of disputing the wishes of my Father, so I must accept that Myra and her sister are the rightful beneficiaries of their Mother's assets.'

The solicitor smiled at them both.

'I believe that neither Myra nor you want to take this to a Court of Law which is expensive and time consuming. This type of battle could only end up alienating two people who have honourable intentions. Despite what you have acknowledged John, Myra does not want to sell your family home either. As I see it, you have two options.'

'One is that you could sell the property, split the proceeds amongst you, or you could lease or rent it, deriving a small income, but still retaining the ownership of a valuable piece of real estate.'

Silence greeted this revelation as it was something that neither of them had considered. The solicitor continued.

'If you do make the latter choice, there are many avenues today which protect your investment about which I would be happy to discuss. Just let me know when you have decided.'

Driving back John seemed relaxed and almost pleased about the situation. Although he had not considered the idea about a shared income from the flat, it was a generous outcome which made a great deal of sense. Myra opened the subject.

'I was surprised at the suggestion made by the Solicitor, but I wouldn't be too happy about trying to sell this property quickly. The proceeds from Mum's Australian house will give me enough to buy a small flat and Jill will use her share against their mortgage.

As you already own your own flat in South Africa, I assume that you would feel the same way? After you confirmed that you don't want to contest your Father's will, it leaves the way open for this to be a better outcome for us both.'

Myra continued. 'We both know that a court case would not only eat in the value of the estate but it would also leave us bitter opponents and I couldn't stand that.'

John sensed that Myra was being totally honest about her beliefs so it was up to him to do the same. As he parked the car in the garage he knew that it was about time that he made up his mind about his future and Myra.

CHAPTER THREE

Merv does some Forward Thinking

Ikey now employed Archie full time, and it proved to be a wonderful partnership. Ikey had a wife but no children so he treated Archie as a son. Merv and Archie were given free accommodation over the shop where Merv worked as a caretaker and cleaner. Ikey always read the newspapers in the shop as it gave him something to talk about and sometimes something to learn. He took great delight in spouting his knowledge about everything.

'Cor lumme this Coronation is going to cost four million pounds for one day's ceremony. Unbelievable! Queen Elizabeth is already Queen of the United Kingdom, Canada, Australia, New Zealand, Ceylon and Pakistan and has taken on the role of Head of Commonwealth. She sure has a lot on her shoulders.'

'Yeah,' said Archie. I knows wot you mean Ikey. That crarn must weigh a tun.'

Ikey smiled. Despite his cockney accent being a little hard to take at times, Ikey appreciated that Archie's humour certainly lightened his workload.

'Arch, when you consider that she had to ascend the throne on the death of her Father, King George the Sixth who died in February 1952, she was still a young woman. She had to mourn his passing and also to take on all those countries as her role as Head of Commonwealth. That would have taken a lot of courage.'

'Will we close darn for the day? Are you gonna watch the procession?'

'Yes we could close up, go to a good vantage point and yell and wave flags like everyone else. There will be a lot of details in the daily papers from now on including a map of the route taken by the Royal Coach, so I will leave it on the counter for you after I have finished.'

Merv had overheard all that Ikey had said but he couldn't admit that neither Arch nor himself had much schooling and to try to read a newspaper with all those details would be a real battle. The night that the pawnshop had been raided and they all went next door, courtesy of the police, Merv felt that the lady who owned the coffee shop seemed very friendly towards him. He was never one to look a gift horse in the mouth. Perhaps if he did some cleaning for her, she might give him some reading lessons. It was worth a try wasn't it?

CHAPTER FOUR

Myra's Feelings are Put on Hold

That evening after dinner John joined Myra in the drawing room. He began.

'How do you feel about renting or leasing this property?'

Myra answered honestly.

'I believe that it would be the right thing to do in the best interests of us all.'

'OK, I think that we should get a value appraisal first and then put it into the hands of a respectable real estate firm. Do you agree?'

Myra smiled at his stern expression which had once turned her off.

'I don't think that this is really a big deal, but I would like you to take charge of all the details regarding the property transaction with the exception of one.'

His expression changed and softened. 'Yes Myra, what is that?'

'When it comes to the income derived from the rental of this lovely old building, I want it written into the contract that the monies have to be split three ways. It is only fair that Jill is included in what would have been the case if Mum had written a new will here in England.'

John gave her a dazzling smile, before he continued.

'If you are sure that this is what you really want I will get on to it tomorrow. It shouldn't take too long. After the Coronation is over, I intend to return home. What about you?'

No matter what thoughts Myra had about John, he was all business. There was another option, but it was not up to her to make the first move in that direction.

'Yes, I will do the same. Tomorrow I shall book my flight and as soon as the crowds have all gone, I will be on my way.'

They both stood to leave. John put his hand on her shoulder as if to delay her but he was not expecting the fire which blazed in her eyes. Before he knew it, he was passionately kissing her and she responded in the same way. Once again he pulled away, holding her as he searched her face.

'Myra, you must know how I feel about you, but I don't want to do anything that would hurt or confuse you. If I am misjudging the situation, I will be the first to admit it, but if this is only a shared emotional experience after our loss, I would be stupid to take advantage of it.'

Myra had no answer to this. She heaved a sigh but said nothing. What was there to say after such an admission of his feelings? The next morning Myra concentrated on shopping for souvenirs to take home for Jill and her family. It was no fun as the shops were crowded but at least it kept her focused on something else beside John

When she arrived back, he was busy with paperwork. There was a tenant ready to move in as soon as the flat was vacant. This man was a foreign diplomat with impeccable credentials and was looking for temporary residence in Mayfair. Myra was happy to sign the contract and to get this all wrapped up in time for the Coronation which was due in three days. John had also been out looking for a good vantage point to view the Coronation Procession.

'I haven't been able to get any tickets in the erected stands close to Piccadilly, but we can still choose from Park Lane, Hyde Park or Marble Arch. What do you think?'

MYRA'S FEELINGS ARE PUT ON HOLD

Myra once again sighed inwardly, but John was making every effort to include her in this wonderful occasion.

'That sounds great. As much as I would love to see the actual crowning of Queen Elizabeth, I believe that it is going to be the first Coronation ever to be televised, so I will be happy to watch it later that way. If we get to view the procession and see the Queen inside the Golden Coach, I will be happy enough.'

— CHAPTER FIVE —

Archie Learns a Little

Ikey was really interested in the coming spectacle and made a point of reading the newspaper out aloud to anyone who would take the time to listen.

"The Queen has to get used to the weight of that Crown. She wears it as she goes about her daily business: at her desk, at tea and while reading the newspapers."

'Just imagine her in her twin set and pearls with the Corgis running around and that ruddy great Crown on her head all day. It would be enough to give her a headache. What do you think about that?'

Merv thought a lot about it, especially with that incredible collection of precious stones.

'Does it say wot the crarn is like an' 'ow many jools it 'as?'

'Yes on the next page it describes the Imperial State Crown this way.'

"It is set with 3000 precious stones including 2868 diamonds, 272 pearls, 17 sapphires, 11 emeralds, and 5 rubies. At the front sits the fourth largest cut diamond in the world known as the Cullinan Diamond at 317.40 carats."

'Ta Ikey,' droned Merv. 'It brings tears to me eyes just finking abart it.'

Archie leant on the counter and remembered how close they had been to all those gems, but now he had a different outlook on what he saw as his English heritage. He was looking forward to watching the parade and enjoying the celebrations.

'Ikey, where abarts is the best place to wotch the parade? Dad an me are keen to get a good spot. After all our spoon will be part of the ceremony won't it?'

'I would keep that bit about the spoon under your hat as it were, as there could be some explaining to do if you get my meaning?' Ikey advised.

'OK I gets your drift, but where are you gonna watch it?'

'Good question my boy. My old legs are not really up to long walks and jostling for a bird's eye view that I can watch in comfort on a TV screen. Your Dad probably hasn't mentioned it but he has become quite friendly with Flo next door. She has kindly invited us to view the whole thing there.

Perhaps you could join us too. Better sort it out with your Dad.'

'Ok Dad, wot's going on? Ave you got sumpin speshall going on wiv Flo?'

Merv blushed before he answered.

'Er, wots that?'

'You eard me. Ow come you are wotching the Coronation on the telly next door?'

'Oh that, well Arch it wos gonna be a surprise an all, but I ave been having sum lessens from Flo and she invited us to see the whole thing on the TV in her shop. That's all.'

'Ok fess up wot kinda lessens is she givin? I know that she is a single lady, but ow close are you and what's this abart a surprise?'

'Arch you are now lookin at someone who is learnin to read n' write. That lady Flo is learnin me in exchange for some cleanin that I does for 'er. I wasn't gonna tell you until I could show you 'ow I'm going, but if I does well perhaps you mite wanta give it a go too.'

'So Dad, are ya gonna see it in the coffee shop or are you gonna see it live like?'

'Well son as I ave been given a personal invite like, it would be rude not to go ya mite say.'

Archie was silent so Ikey took up the newspaper again and read aloud.

'This paper really makes it seem that the Coronation belongs to the people. When it came to the TV broadcast it says, "There has been considerable debate within the British Cabinet on the subject, with Prime Minister Winston Churchill against the idea, but Elizabeth refused her Prime Minister's advice on this matter and insisted that the event take place before television cameras," Ikey informed them.

'Thet's telling 'em. Good fer 'er. She has alreddy begun to consider 'er people like thet. I am pleased that she got 'er special spoon back in time fer all this,' grinned Archie.

Ikey chuckled. 'Arch, call Merv in here. Something has tickled my warped sense of humour and I think he should hear it.'

"Elizabeth will be anointed as the Assembly sings "Zadok the Priest." Then her jewelry and crimson cape will be removed. She will wear only a simple white linen dress and seat herself on the Coronation Chair where she will receive a cross on her forehead with holy oil from the Archbishop. But because this segment of the ceremony is considered absolutely sacrosanct, it will be concealed from view of the television cameras by a silk canopy held above the Queen by four Knights of the Garter."

'So my dear chaps, unless you are sitting in Westminster Abbey with a very good view, you are not going to see your spoon at all. You can be sure that it will be used in the most sacred part of the whole ceremony.'

Merv and Archie were silent as this news sank in. It seemed a just reward for their audacity in taking the spoon in the first place. Merv decided that it was a little bit like a punishment.

'Well I'm glad we took it back. It is so important and sacrud, and we all know thet it will be used in the most important part anyway.'

If anything this episode had touched a chord within Archie which made his appreciation of what was happening in his world come into greater focus. If his Dad was learning to read and write, it wouldn't be a bad idea for him to go to night school and do the same.

'Rite, that is ow it will be. I'm gonna take orf and find a spot thet'll give me a good view and we can compare notes after it's all ova.'

Ikey had one word of warning to Archie.

'There are bound to be people camped in the streets, and there will be scaffolding and bleachers along the route so be very careful where you decide to wait. Have a great day and be sure to tell us all about it when you get back. We will be waiting at the Coffee Shop.'

Archie waved 'bye and left.

— CHAPTER SIX —

Coronation Day

London 1953

On the second of June it was rumoured that nearly three million spectators would gather in the streets of London with 200 microphones stationed along the path and inside Westminster Abbey. 750 Commentators broadcasting descriptions in 39 languages with approximately 20 million viewers around the world would be watching the coverage.

John and Myra left at dawn with many thousands of spectators until they found a suitable gap where they could see the procession. This site allowed an uninterrupted view as the excitement preceded the passing of the Gold State Coach with a roar that was deafening. Unfortunately when a group surged forward to get a better view, Myra felt herself being pushed forward with tremendous force. With all the noise her cries went unheeded. When John saw her slip underneath the crowd, he couldn't get to her in time. After the Gold Coach carrying Her Majesty had moved on, he managed to reach her, but she was unconscious. An ambulance was summoned and carried Myra to a nearby hospital. John was devastated about this terrible accident but was somewhat relieved when the Doctor assured him that Myra had slight concussion, and apart from two black eyes, would come through it.

Seated on a chair beside her bed, John murmured.

'My dearest Myra, I don't know what I would have done if you had been harmed. When we get over this nightmare, I am going to ask you to marry me.'

Myra winced as she tried to take hold of his hand.

'What's wrong with now, or are you afraid that my promised black eyes will make me look like a vampire?'

She was right. What was wrong with right now?

On his knees, he asked the question just as the Doctor approached the bed.

'Myra, I love you. Will you do me the honour of becoming my wife?'

'Yes of course I will.' Myra replied. 'I love you too.'

The doctor gently lifted John up by his elbow, telling him that Matron had a thing about highly polished floors.

CORONATION DAY

'We don't want another patient, so perhaps you had better sit on that chair and kiss the lady from there.' Very gently, John found her lips. When he finished kissing her, John began to make wedding plans.

'Don't be in such a hurry my love. There is much to discuss. After all I have to shop for a trousseau and I am certainly not going out looking as if my fiancée has just beaten me up,' she replied.

'You are quite right of course. Anyone who could disguise herself to look like the Fat Lady from the circus and return a spoon to the London Tower certainly deserves my complete understanding on these matters.'

'And anyone who could tell me that he can admire a beautiful Edwardian toilet suite after I have just stabbed him with my stiletto shoe certainly deserves my complete adoration,' said Myra.

'How do you feel about living in South Africa? The Museum has been very considerate with me but I have already used up my compassionate leave after the deaths of our parents.'

'As long as I am with you it can be Timbuktu as far as I am concerned, but I do want our wedding to take place in Australia.' He laughed at her reference to that town.

'That place really does exist, but I can see by your expression that I had better introduce you to the wilds of Africa very slowly.'

The next day he collected Myra from the hospital. She still had purple bruises on both cheeks and two black half moons beneath her eyes, but John was overjoyed to have her safely home so he began to make plans for their flight home. Myra commenced with her own ideas.

'Whilst I was in hospital, I gave this matter a bit of thought which I want to discuss with you. I do want to marry you as I have loved you for some time, but I don't want to rush into anything too quickly.'

'Yes Myra there are some loose ends which need attention. We have to consider that this flat will be occupied by a foreign diplomat very soon. Thankfully he is happy to take it fully furnished but we can postpone his occupancy for a little while. The fact that you have had this accident and that you have not yet fully recovered from the fall will be enough for the postponement.'

Myra was tired and exhausted, but she didn't sleep immediately. She was happy and excited about their future plans but she also needed to contact Jill with the news. There was a wedding to be planned in Australia. Her eyes filled with tears as she considered that the sale of their Mother's house also had to be arranged. With all these thoughts fluttering around in her mind like a swarm of bees, Myra eventually drifted off.

The next morning John brought her a breakfast tray and discussed his busy morning. He was going to book their delayed flights to Australia, which should give Myra the time she needed. When this was confirmed he would visit the real estate to inform them that the property would not be vacant before that date. Myra listened with a frown.

'It all sounds good, but a fortnight seems such a short time. Do you think that I will be able to fly by then? It isn't likely that we will return to England for some time so I would like to visit the pawn shop and say farewell to those two men who helped me return the 'Spoon' to the Tower and most importantly I want to make a visit to the Cemetery to say goodbye to Mum and David.'

After ringing Ikey and informing him of their impending visit, and despite her obvious discomfort, John managed to help Myra into the car. When she arrived, her eyes opened wide at the sight of Merv and Archie. Merv was wearing a long clean white apron almost down to his ankles and of all things a cravat! Archie seemed to have an air of confidence about him, but he still managed a shy smile for Myra. (He thought that she was a bit of all right).

Ikey did not dwell on the subject of their sad loss, but he was quite entranced by Myra's good looks as well as her initiative shown in returning the Spoon to the Tower. Myra was positive in her comments to Merv and Archie now that they both had steady jobs with Ikey, and she was interested in their opinion of the Coronation.

'Talk about being disappointed,' said Archie. 'I got a reel surprise when Ikey tole me that the Anointeng was done in secret. Some geysers put a canopy over 'er to ide 'er from the cameras. If ya ask me that ole Archbishop probably couldn't see if that spoon was the propa one, or even if it was a repulca.'

Loud laughter from everyone but John replied.

'Yes Arch, you have a point there, but hopefully they found the 'real' one before the Coronation. They would have taken special care to make sure about that. Anyway we have a special announcement to make of our own.

Myra and I have become engaged and we will be flying back to Australia next week.'

'Wonderful news. Congratulations, said Ikey. 'Let's have a toast. Archie, go out to the back of the shop and bring in those bottles of beer that are there. It should really be wine or champagne, but if we drunk that sort of stuff, these coves would be history, and I still need them to work today.'

Myra didn't even like beer, let alone warm beer served in cloudy glasses, but she wouldn't hurt Ikey's feelings, so she managed to drink a little. John turned to Ikey.

'Thank you for those kind words and before we leave England, we would like to give you some of the contents of the Mayfair flat to sell at your own discretion. The furniture will remain for the tenants, but there are lots of small items that we do not want to take with us. I can promise that there are no anointing spoons amongst them.'

Ikey was happy that John was to leave some of the contents for him to sell, and he told John that after Archie noted the items down, they would do their best to sell them. Myra promised to come back and say a final goodbye when John delivered the goods to them. After they returned to the flat, it was time to pack their own belongings and to sort out the shelves and cupboards which needed to be boxed for Ikey. At last John announced that it was done. Myra asked.

'What about the cupboard under the stairs?'

'What cupboard under the stairs? I have never noticed that there was one there.'

CHAPTER SEVEN

Hidden Silver

'The other day when I was limping about down here, I lost my balance and fell against the wood paneling and part of it gave way. I think that it must be some kind of magnetic catch because there is no visible sign of a knob or anything else to open the door.'

'It must be a broom or storage cupboard. Did you switch on the light?

'No,' Myra replied. 'I couldn't see any switch.'

'Ok, I'll find a torch and we can investigate this mysterious cupboard.'

When John found the torch, he pushed against the section which Myra indicated. Coming face to face with a lot of old dusty items such a set of golf clubs, a folding up chair, piles of magazines and stacks of newspapers, he was not very impressed with the contents which obviously had been undisturbed for years. He moved towards the back of the cupboard and realized that there were many cardboard boxes stacked on top of each other, also covered with dust. Placing the torch down on top of one of them, he opened the nearest box. For a minute John was speechless. Then he muttered.

'The sly old fox, I should have known. Anointing spoons were only part of his interest in 'Old Silver.' He backed out slowly and smiled at Myra.

'This cupboard is full of junk and old papers but they are only a smokescreen to hide what is hidden at the back of it. There are dozens of large cardboard boxes all containing his real fortune. I have opened one only which holds smaller boxes with exquisite antique pieces in them. This stash would represent many years of collecting of what must be another small fortune, but sadly we have so little time to decide what to do with all this.'

'Oh, John please show them to me. This sounds like 'Aladdin's Cave,' but I can't understand why they were not listed in your Father's will.'

'Who knows what went through his mind? Don't go in there. There is so much stuff lying around and I can't have you falling or slipping again. I will bring them out to you.' As John moved into the cupboard, his Father's will preyed on his mind again. Was it possible that David hoped that Myra's Mother would be instrumental in bringing him and Myra together when this discovery was made? After all, the rest of the house contents, were not specifically mentioned in the will. If Vanessa was to become a widow and did find them she would surely contact John as this was once his Father's house and John was a Museum Curator with knowledge about such antiques. These were all unanswerable questions, but they went a long way to explain why his Father was so secretive and perhaps even cunningly underhanded?

When John carried out a box, he placed it on the coffee table in the drawing room. Myra could not contain her curiosity as John lifted out a smaller elongated leather box. A strange object lay within the satin lining.

'Whatever is that? She asked. He grinned with recollection.

'I remember this. It is an Asparagus Tong used for grasping and straining asparagus. It is part of Dad's collection of Antique Silver Flatware and there would be other flatware contained in these boxes.'

'Asparagus Tong? We only ate them from a can. Posh restaurants cooked and served them fresh, but we are looking at a different era I guess. Please open another small box. I need to know a little more about flatware.' John obliged.

'Well in this box we have some more silver spoons, such as a Berry spoon, a Tea Caddy spoon, a Marrow spoon, a Medicine spoon and I think this one is a Mote spoon.'

'Whatever is a Mote spoon?'

'As it looks a little like a strainer, it would have been used to remove any floaties on the surface of the tea. The pointed end looks lethal, and I guess that it was used to dislodge blockages from the teapot's spout.'

'All that trouble just for a cup of tea?'

'Yes my love, taking tea was once a time honoured ritual, not like today's quick sip, but our biggest problem is what to do with all of this. We cannot dispose or sell them or even store them in such a short space of time.'

'This is just a suggestion, but could we ask Ikey to give us an appraisal and even perhaps catalogue them?'

'I can't see how that would work. There is too many and too much value for him to store and possibly too difficult for us to ship to Cape Town. In the meantime I am going to haul out all these boxes and we can see what we have to contend with. I am loathe to put any pressure on Ikey after what he has already been through, but he has proven trustworthy, so perhaps a phone call might be in order.'

Ikey was more than pleased to come over with Archie and Myra told John to invite them both for tea before they got down to business. Ikey's head swum as his eyes appreciated the elegant décor. Archie's eyes nearly popped out of his head, looking at things which he had only seen in posh magazines. Myra poured tea from a teapot and handed around some dainty sandwiches on a plate. Archie thanked her after taking the whole plate. She said nothing but went outside into the kitchen where she had some reserves. Telling herself that she should have known better. Both men would have good appetites. After supper was completed John spoke to Ikey.

'In the hallway near the stairs there are some cardboard boxes with a very valuable collection of Antique Silver which belonged to my Dad and also to Myra's Mother. Our problem is that we are not sure about how we should handle them.'

'What are in these boxes?' Ikey moved towards them to have a closer look. 'Blimey, look at all this! I believe that I am looking at a 'Moustache Spoon' and that's a 'Runcible Spoon, and a Snuff box Spoon, a cheese scoop, a sugar sifter, sugar tongs and tea tongs. This is incredible! Wait, please don't show me any more. I can see that this is a valuable and comprehensive collection, and you have only shown me a small percentage of what must be in those other boxes. This has taken my breath away, just looking at them, but it would be too dangerous for me to handle such valuable objects in my pawn shop. I could take a few lesser pieces, but in all faith, sadly there seems too much for me to consider.' With his hands behind his back, Archie cleared his throat and spoke with confidence.

'Cor Mr. Collins, this is top clobber. I can only relate this tressure with wot Dad an' me saw in the Tower. Perhaps it belongs in a museum.'

John's expression took on a look of quiet respect as he considered that Arch may have just hit on the answer. After all he was a curator of the Cape Town Museum and as such he could ship these items if he had permission from his superiors. They could be on loan but Myra and he would still retain the ownership.

'Arch, you're a genius. That would be the best outcome for us all. Myra and I will do a quick inventory, and then find a reputable shipping agent to ship most of this to South Africa. We might just keep a few small pieces as Wedding gifts.' When John realized that he would not be leaving any of the Antique Silver with Ikey to sell, he insisted on loading up his car with the smaller household items which he had promised Ikey.

'These are yours to sell. We can't take them with us and it would make us happy to know that you will get some benefit from these items. Please share the sales evenly amongst yourself, Merv and Archie.' The next morning Merv was astounded at the 'haul' that greeted his eyes.

'Lumme Ikey, this is good clobber. Jus look at this china. It says 'Royal Doulton.' What about thet.' Archie held up some lovely figurines and some Stuart crystal vases, with something akin to wonder, but

Ikey's favourite was the Wedgwood Collection. He knew his missus would have her eyes on these.

'Cor, luv a duck,' said Merv. 'Are ya gonna put all this in the pawn shop? We doan ave eny alarms and it mite be a bit foolish if ya doan miond me saying so.'

'I'm glad that you think along those lines Merv, because I believe that it is time that we branched out. There is an antique shop for sale in Portobello Road that would suit us fine. I've saved a little money over the years, enough for a deposit so I'm going to make an offer today. It has good security and large living quarters above the shop.'

'Great idea,' piped up Archie. 'Then me and Dad can 'ave separate bedrooms.' Merv grimaced before he answered his son.

'Doan be too 'astie, this is not appening overnite and I may 'ave some plans of me own.'

'Eh, wotcha mean Dad?'

'Well me an Flo as been seeing a lot of each other, an she is needing a man to 'elp out in the coffee shop like. If she accepts, I'm thinking of tying the knot.' Ikey slapped his thigh with joy, whilst Archie blinked a few times as this news sank in.

'So ya wouldn't be wif us in the pawn shop anymore?'

'Nah Arch, if she wants to be me missus, I couldn't elp out ere as well as in next door. It wouldn't be proppa like.' Ikey was so happy for Merv, but he needed a partner who was strong and reliable, and Arch seemed to fit the bill. His wife rarely came into the shop. She often complained of feeling poorly. Ikey, full of enthusiasm departed to negotiate the possible sale of the Antique shop.

Meanwhile Myra and John were still sorting and listing the contents of the boxes, when she came across some silver basting spoons.

'My goodness, I don't believe it. These spoons are so much like the one that I have at home. I wonder if your Father realised that when he saw it?

'What spoon are we discussing now?'

'Because we have been so busy I forgot to mention it, but your Dad showed some interest in a Silver Spoon that came into my possession when he came out to Australia. I'll show it you when we return.'

'Well my poppet, just to put you into the picture, I have phoned Cape Town about this shipment and I am just waiting for confirmation. I know that we have the original smaller boxes with their contents, but we don't have the original boxes for the larger items. The serving trays, tea and coffee sets and candlesticks will have to be packed very carefully into larger containers.'

'There are so many beautiful pieces, but I would like to put some aside for our personal use if you are agreeable. I will leave them in a box on the kitchen table.' John studied the contents for a minute or two.

'You have wonderful taste. A silver tray, four silver candlesticks, a tankard, a pair of covered gravy boats, a coffee pot, a teapot, sugar bowl and creamer, salt and pepper shakers, a small fruit bowl, four serviette rings and the Rococo Silver-Gilt cup with its lid. I couldn't have picked a better selection myself.'

'I'm glad you approve. I have included four candlesticks because two are for Jill and Brian.' John put his arms around her and kissed her tenderly, having to disentangle himself when the phone rang. It was Ikey.

CHAPTER EIGHT

Good News and Good Byes

"Mr. Collins, I have some good news. I am negotiating the sale with the owner of an antique shop, and so far it is looking good. Now that I have some wonderful pieces, thanks to your generosity as well as a few nondescript items in the pawn shop, I will be able to set us up nicely. The owner wants to get out and retire but he strikes a hard bargain.'

'Ikey you must call me John, and might I suggest that you offer a sweetener? Sometimes it will clinch the deal.'

'I'm not too sure what you mean. Should I offer him something else as well as money?"

'Yes, certainly! Does he have a wife? If you were to ask this man if you might have a word with her and bring along the Wedgwood Collection, which is quite valuable, she may just swing the result in your favour. This of course is only to be handed over when you come to an agreed price. This would be a lovely gift and a collection which could be added to over the years. Most women like to collect things. Don't you agree?

'Are you sure you're not Jewish?' Ikey chuckled. 'You would have made a great salesman in our line of business. My only problem is that my wife rather fancies that Wedgwood collection herself. How can I talk her out of it?'

'I haven't got any more bargaining chips left, but you might. When did you last take your wife on a holiday?'

'A holiday? We haven't had one for years. She does have a sister in Brighton, and I suppose that she would like to visit her, but how can I forget about the Wedgwood?'

'Simple. Just don't tell her about it. When your sale comes through, tell her that because she is always feeling poorly you have decided to take her to visit her sister in Brighton. This should lift her spirits. Merv and Arch could mind the shop while you are away. If this sale goes through and your wife enquires about the Wedgwood, tell her the truth, which is that the Antique shop owner and his wife insisted that the collection was part of the asking price. Of most importance, buy the missus a nice piece of Wedgwood and make sure that you add to it on every occasion that you can.' John hung up leaving a rather nervous caller on the other end but Ikey was feeling more confident now. Business was business.

After he had received the confirmation from Cape Town that the insurance had been covered, with Myra's help they completed the Inventory. John supervised the packing which was done by a recommended firm. There was little left to do except say their goodbyes.

The first place was the cemetery. The loss they felt was as strong as the bond that bound them as they held hands at the graveside. Silently they made their farewells.

The next stop was the pawn shop where the smile on Ikey's face told them that the news was good. Even Ikey's missus came to say goodbye and announced that her husband was taking her on a holiday. Arch and Merv were lined up looking so spic and span that Myra couldn't help herself. She kissed each one on the cheek and whispered,

'Goodbye, my partners in crime.' From behind the counter Ikey produced a small parcel and said,

'At great expense and time consuming effort we would like you both to accept this Wedding Gift from us all.'

'Oh, John, look at this,' grinned Myra. Inside a lovely new box lay a small replica of a Coronation Spoon.

'Thank you all. This is something that we will always cherish. There are powerful memories attached to it, so we will use it constantly and think of you.' With handshakes all around, and a glistening eye from Ikey, John and Myra walked out of the pawn shop for the last time.

— CHAPTER NINE —

A Wedding

Australia 1953

Jill and Brian were there to meet the plane. There was much excitement as Jill insisted that they all share dinner that night to discuss the wedding plans. She knew that her sister and her fiancée would not be staying long in Australia and she wanted the arrangements to be perfect for Myra. Jill told Myra that their Mother's house had been listed for sale with a real estate company. After dinner Myra presented Jill and Brian with a pair of Silver Antique candlesticks. At the back of her mind Myra did recall Jill's comments about old Silver so she pre-empted any comment from Jill by saying,

'These antique pieces are very old and quite valuable, and we have the matching pair, so use and enjoy them. Believe me they will be much admired by anyone who lays eyes on them. Just don't forget to lock up your silver.' Both Jill and Brian were thrilled by this lovely gift.

The next day Jill and Myra went to book the Church. When this was done, the venue for the reception was next. Myra wanted it to be an early evening affair in a Marquee on the beach. This was arranged but the Wedding dress took a little more time. Myra wanted to buy one off the rack. She tried on a creation which brought sighs of raptures from Jill, but Myra thought it too fancy. Eventually she found just what she was looking for. It reminded her of the simple white silk dress worn by the Queen at her Coronation without the precious stones. Myra chose Ballerina length, slightly full skirted with capped sleeves, reflecting with a soft shine the glow from Myra's face. A short fingertip veil would be held in place by a circle of white roses also included in her bouquet. Myra turned to Jill and confessed.

'I can't wait to be married. I am so much in love. John is an amazing man and although we spent more time in England that we anticipated, he has to be back at work in South Africa after taking off all that extra time. As long as I am with him, it won't matter where we live.'

'Today has been wonderful, and although I wish that you were settling in Australia, I understand your feelings all too well when I see the love that you have for each other.' Jill freely admitted.

This comment brought tears to Myra as she realised that she would be parted from her sister for a long time. This was another life altering moment. She hugged Jill silently recalling that they both had been through some tragic experiences, but these were shared as only sisters can.

'I would like to ask your daughter Frances to be my flower girl and of course to have you as my Matron of honour. Nan's neighbour Marjorie is quite elderly but I'm sure that she would be pleased to get an invitation. As John has no siblings or parents, this will be a small gathering. I have invited a few of my journalist friends, but it will be more like a family gathering.'

The night before the wedding and keeping to tradition, Myra left her sister's home where she and John had been staying and went back to her flat. This is where she would leave from with Jill and Frances in the late afternoon. She needed to do some packing for her flight to Cape Town. This included her old Silver Spoon.

'Another chapter of my life and you will be sharing it with me,' she whispered. 'Who knows what your inscription will reveal, but I know that I will make the time to find out.'

Myra looked radiantly beautiful. Her happiness knew no bounds as she was escorted down the aisle by Brian. Jill and Frances were dressed in pale blue chiffon with a pearl choker around their necks. As they repeated their vows to each other, the expression of unconditional love shone on John's face. Myra knew that she was truly blessed. As they were leaving the Church, an old lady came towards them. It was Marjorie. She pressed a small parcel into Myra's hands, saying.

'Thanks for your kind invitation. I am so happy to see the happiness in your eyes, but I could only stay for the ceremony. Goodbye and good luck.'

Myra assured her husband that she would tell him about Marjorie at a later date. Meanwhile she told him.

'Our reception is going to be such a small gathering but this is my home town and I want to share some of its natural beauty with you.'

'At the risk of sounding unoriginal, I am standing with a natural beauty whom I have just wed, but as this is your special day, lead on my lovely wife.'

After dusk the small marquee glowed with the lights of many candles. Myra had managed to find some Proteas, and she intertwined them with sprigs of golden wattle. The floral emblem of South Africa was recognised by John as he appreciated what Myra had chosen to silently say with flowers. Turning to face Myra, he stood to make a speech.

'In a very short time Myra and I have shared more ups and downs than I would have wished, but knowing that life is like that, I want to share every day of my life with you beside me. I love you.'

A WEDDING

Although he kissed Myra with great solemnity for as long as was suitable at a Wedding, cheers and whistles erupted.

'I would also like to compliment the Matron of Honour Jill, her husband Brian and their daughter Frances, and all who helped to make tonight such a special occasion. Please eat and enjoy our Wedding Breakfast.'

The meal served was not typically Australian because as Myra explained, steaks and a barbecue were not possible in this palace of white fabric, but the substitution of Beef Wellington was more than appreciated. This was followed by Pavlova dessert with flaming eggshells in their centre. After that and a few glasses of wine, the conversation became louder. It was time for John and Myra to slip away. Outside the stars were shining like all the silver in the world was saluting them with their own personal wedding canopy. Myra took John's hand and began to drag him away from the tent.

'This way my darling, I want to walk barefoot with you in the moonlight along the water's edge and feel every step we take that leads us to our new life together. This is where life originally began and I want to make my mark tonight starting now.'

John kissed her again. As surprised as he was about her passionate declaration, he knew that Myra was capable of such depths of feeling and he was more than willing to comply. He followed her lead as she removed her shoes and they ran like two children chasing the waves together in the starlight. Their kisses became more urgent and John knew that it was time to leave.

Hailing a taxi, he gave the name of the Hotel Australia where he had booked for their Wedding night. The taxi driver took in their disheveled state, bare feet and signs of lipstick smeared all over each other's faces. She was wearing a dress that was wet and sandy. He wondered why they were even bothering with a room at all. From time to time he glanced into the rear view mirror where the two newlyweds were still wrapped in each other. Serious doubts arose as to whether he would get them there in time.

Once inside, John gave their names for the reservation, received the key and hurried to their suite. This is where Myra wanted to be and what she had waited for. John quickly undressed her, but she was laughing so much where the wet sandy dress stuck to her legs and then to her arms as he hoisted it over her head. As soon as they fell onto the bed her laughing ceased. This was serious business. Although she knew what to expect, Myra was a virgin.

When that hurdle was over they moved in perfect harmony as if it was their second nature. Myra's eyes flew open in surprise as she felt John inside her in a way that she could never have imagined. This must be what is known as two becoming one. She was as passionate as her husband and needed to enjoy everything that she had so long denied herself. This new experience made her feel alive with the awareness of physical love in every part of her trembling body. After some time they both fell into a light slumber, but Myra eventually awoke as she felt his hand caressing her breast. She groaned with delight, turning her body towards him as he covered her with his own.

Again she felt the movement of the seashore. This is how life began. She felt it deep in her soul. John controlled the rhythm, but the melody sung in her head as she welcomed this awakening. By now her legs were shaking with weakness. She had lost control over her body which no longer belonged to her. She sat up and looked into John's eyes.

'My darling, I am ravenous. Would you please order me a jumbo sized breakfast in half an hour? First I am going to take a long bath, but after that my dearest husband, I will be in need of nourishment.'

After she had bathed and eaten Myra felt her body was tender in certain places. Perhaps it would be wiser to take this love making a little more slowly. John came over to where she was sitting.

'How are you feeling my dearest? This was something completely new to you and I want to know if you are still the beautiful lady who seduced me last night on the sandy shore.' Myra took hold of his hand.

'I am still tingling all over but there are no complaints from me. This condition had better subside as we go through married life or I will be hopelessly and helplessly in love forever. How long does this feeling last?'

'As long as we are madly in love I don't care and I can't answer about the female sensations that you describe. I believe that this will change a little as we grow older but for now it is great to hear you talk this way, my beloved Mrs. Collins.'

That morning Brian arrived to collect them. There was little time to spare before their departure the following day, but an Aussie barbecue had been organised complete with flies and a few bottles of cold beer. John told Brian about the three-way split from the rental property in London and the fact that this would be paid monthly into their joint account. Brian also confirmed that the sale of Vanessa's Australian house was in the pipeline and that he would keep in touch with the details. The two sisters hugged each other at the airport, before the tears began. The children couldn't understand why this was happening so they began to bawl when they saw their Mother crying. John smiled at this scene, but their flight had been called, so a quick goodbye was the best way. It was time to board.

CHAPTER TEN

Jamie's Letters

The plane took off. Myra was on the last leg of this amazing journey to her new home. The 'fasten your seat-belt light' came off, so she reached for her hand luggage to remove a small parcel. This was really the first opportunity that Myra had to explain to John about Marjorie and the package that she received after their wedding. It was an old square tin with faded words which were impossible to identify. Marjorie had put a note on the top of what looked like very old letters.

"My dear Myra, I was happy to hear that you were to be married, but I also knew that it was not likely that I would ever see you again. Despite the fact that I hoped for another visit from you, it never happened. I know that you have been busy just getting on with your own life, so I do understand. After I had given your Nan's diary to you, I realised that I had still another piece of this tragic story, and I hoped that you might be interested in hearing more. I am now quite the invalid and if time is not kind to me, I have to face the fact that my days are numbered. That is why I know that I am doing the right thing in giving this to you. Keep well and happy.

Marjorie."

Shivering in spite of herself, Myra knew that these were letters that once belonged to Laura. She was also aware that they were an intrusion on someone's personal life, but after having read Nan's diary, this was much the same. If Marjorie had given them to her, it must have been with her blessing. They were bound by old faded ribbon and she instinctively knew that they were love letters from Jamie.

The first letter was full of enthusiasm and bravado. His fellow soldiers were all good chaps, blessed with laconic humour. Most of them considered that the war would be over too soon and they would not be able to make a good job of it. The next one was a little more sombre. (Myra felt that perhaps Jamie had lost some of his mates), but it was also full of endearments which a young man might send to his sweetheart.

The third letter began with desperate words of love and longing, hinting that this war was going to be long and difficult. Would she please wait for him? Myra now read the fourth letter with sympathy as she could see how it must have affected Laura.

"My dearest Laura, I have to face the possibility that I may never return to the one that I love most in this world. You are and always will be the reason for my happiness, and I will treasure the time that we spent together. I know that you feel the same way about me but if we cannot renew our love, please do not think that I am being cowardly about this war, which is cruel, dirty and at times seems hopeless. So many of my comrades have fallen with numbers that seem horrific and unending. Because of this, I have to talk about the old Silver Spoon which I gave to you before I left to fight this war.

Although it has my initials, this spoon has been in my family for many years and handed down through the generations of the Christie family. My Dad (Joel) told me that it had been passed down from Jack Christie who was given it by an old shipmate who had served with him under Captain James Cook on the 'Endeavour.' So you see my dearest, this is a wonderful souvenir of a special time in history. As it was the only item of value that I owned, I wanted to give it to the woman that I love. Forever yours, Jamie."

Myra knew that the pieces had all fallen into place and now she had some of the names which were attached to the spoon's provenance. Once again she felt a tug of emotion as she re-tied the letters and returned them to the old tin. John had watched the change on Myra's face from curiosity to an expression of sorrow. He wanted to know what these letters were all about as he realised that her eyes were brimming with tears.

'I won't show these to you now, but when we arrive and have settled into our new home I will explain in detail how these relate to an old silver spoon which I found in my Nan's kitchen drawer. Your Father showed some interest in it when he was in Australia. For now my darling, just hold my hand and help me to appreciate how lucky I am to be married to you.'

When the plane arrived, the newly wed couple was met by two of John's colleagues, who were so happy to welcome Myra and assist John with the luggage. John appreciated their kind efforts, but as soon as they were alone he told Myra that although he had a double bed, his flat was unsuitable for two people, they would have to find a small house as soon as possible. Myra was invited to morning teas and luncheons to meet and get to know everybody. She soon became a popular visitor while John tried to catch up on his work backlog. If he was busy at work, he couldn't wait to get home to Myra who never tired of his affection as they settled down into married life.

Eventually John found a modest cottage which Myra decorated with new curtains and cushions. It was bright, clean, cheerful and just big enough to be cosy and comfortable. After all her things were unpacked, it felt like home at last. She waited until

John arrived home that night and then produced her spoon for his attention.

'Do you remember the old spoon which we discussed in London and on the plane coming here? Well here it is.' John held it for a few seconds before turning it over to read the hallmarks.

'Yes I do recall our short discussions but I had no idea just how old it was or that it had initials and a Latin Motto. It could be Hanoverian Silver, but I will have to get hold of a Hallmark identity book that could date this.'

'Fine, I have waited for quite some time to identify it. If I have to wait a little longer, it won't really matter. Speaking of time, when is our shipment due to arrive from London?'

'Not for another few weeks I have been told, but in the meantime I have been so busy catching up on all the Museum's exhibits, so I have not noticed the time dragging.'

'I have to do some shopping tomorrow, and I thought that I might come by the Museum and have some lunch with you. It would give me the opportunity to do a little pottering around at my leisure.'

'That would be great. There is so much to see. Just don't get lost.'

CHAPTER ELEVEN

A Beginning and an End

When Myra arrived the next day she became so engrossed in the many displays that she really didn't notice the time passing until John found her to take her to lunch. He seemed mildly excited.

'We are about to host an exhibition here very soon which has come from Australia and it includes a selection of flatware and cutlery according to the inventory. The illustrated silver spoons look to be very similar to the one in your possession, but the most significant thing about this collection is the fact that it includes mementos of Captain Cook.'

Myra held her sandwich in mid-air as she felt a shiver of excitement run down her back.

'But John the initials on my spoon are J.C. What else is included and why would this exhibit come here?

'Not so fast my poppet. I haven't unpacked it yet and there is much to do before it can be put on display. All I can tell you is that it came from Cooktown in Queensland, and that Captain Cook after running his ship aground on some coral reefs in Cape Tribulation sought shelter of the beaches in what is now Cooktown. According to the manifesto, he spent 48 days there repairing his ship, The Endeavour.'

'Wow, I can understand why museums are keen to share their artefacts around the world, but why come here to South Africa?'

'My dear wife, didn't you learn about him at school? He had a stopover in Cape Town for water and provisions, but that is not the only reason. I will relate what the accompanying leaflet recommends. It goes something like this. "Cultural development is traced through artefacts which can be as diverse as rock painting and stone implements, and also by items brought back from the Pacific Islands by the explorer Captain James Cook."

'Ok, so the cultural sharing of these artefacts seems to relate to a different category to those which apply to silverware. I'm probably missing something here. Are these other items also part of the memorabilia included in this shipment?'

'Come with me my curious one. Let's go to my office where we can read about them in detail.' Picking up the inventory, John read out aloud.

'Apart from the pieces that came from the Pacific Islands there are cherished mementos from his widow Elizabeth. These include his dress sword, shoe buckles, his Bible and a waistcoat made from Tahitian tapa cloth which she never finished because he didn't return from that fateful voyage. This is all very interesting but Myra, so is your spoon. I suggest that you bring it with you tomorrow and I will ask a colleague to give us his opinion about it.'

John's colleague, James Robertson was very interested. He knew a lot about Captain James Cook. He believed that the Motto and Crest were positive indicators to the ownership but the sterling silver hallmarks were a little confusing and needed some clarification before he could comment.

'After examining your spoon I feel that I have to explain my thoughts. Firstly it is hallmarked London 1750, with the maker's initials "E.J.". The handle is engraved with the initials "J.C." These details are on the positive side, but when I researched the maker's initials, I found that there were three London silversmiths with those initials. I considered that Elizabeth Jackson would be the best candidate, and even though she was E.J in 1749, she married in 1750 and became Elizabeth Oldfield. If she made these spoons before she married Mr. Oldfield, the dates do not tie up. However the good news is that I have compared your spoon with the one sent with the 'Cook Exhibit,' and they both have identical Motto and Crest.'

Myra was overjoyed, 'Is there some way that we can investigate these two dates and the different maker's initials?'

James Robertson's eyes twinkled with delight at her enthusiasm, but he cautioned patience. He intended to phone a London colleague who was an authority on such details and he would let her know when he had any further news. John noticed his wife's heightened colour so he said.

'What are you going to do if it is confirmed that this spoon actually did belong to Cook?

'That is a good question. From what I can gather so far, the initials and the dates of 1750 do not match up. If it does turn out to have belonged to Captain Cook, I will be able to tie it to the young man in Nan's diary named James Christie. If I can make a connection it will solve the secret of my silver spoon.'

'Dearest Myra, you have a natural inclination and all the instincts of an historian. I can see why you and I are made for each other. I will be unpacking the artefacts tomorrow, so you can come here and help while you are waiting for the verdict from James Robertson.' Her quest was so close now and she knew by intuition that the crates of Cook memorabilia held much promise. She was more than ready to join her husband's side the next day.

'Myra, use this pair of cotton gloves. Please keep them on at all times when you are handling these items. I am going to begin with the notes referring to Elizabeth Batts of Barking who married Cook in 1762. She lived until 1835 dying at 93 years of age. Amongst her household treasures is an old Bible from which her husband read every Sunday to his crew. He would quote Psalm 119: 105. "Thy word is a lamp unto my feet, and a light unto my path."

With a gloved hand, Myra picked up the Bible, gently turned the pages until she found Psalm 119. It was a fitting message for those at sea. Slowly closing it shut, her eyes were drawn to some of the cloth binding which had frayed and was lying unevenly behind the book's spine. Removing her gloves she tried to push it back but it wouldn't move. She found a magnifying glass and then called to John.

'Come and have a look at this. There seems to be some kind of waxed paper poked into this spine's recess.' John frowned. He wasn't happy to think that Myra was tampering with a precious artefact. After he had inspected the Bible, he gave her a small pair of tweezers as well as her cotton gloves and told her to gently ease out whatever was interfering with the lining of the spine. Carefully Myra removed what seemed to be a small folded card, enclosing a lock of hair. The writing was only just legible.

A BEGINNING AND AN END

"My Dearest Love, please carry this lock of my hair with you always." Myra gasped at this beautiful note of love. The words of Nan's neighbour Marjorie, echoed in her head.

"Lots of things change over the years, but true love never does."

She couldn't help thinking about the long and lonely life which Elizabeth Cook must have had, but here after 180 years a little glimmer of her love still remained. Perhaps she never knew that James had put it there as this was returned to her after Cook had been killed by natives. The little card was something very private and sacred to their memory, so Myra told John that she was replacing where it belonged. He nodded in agreement. The next day James Robertson met John and Myra in the Museum with some good news. According to his London source, some strange occurrences took place re the Date Letter.

'Apart from the fact that each assay office had its own cycle of letters, the date letter changed annually in May. Hence an item described as being made in 1750 theoretically could have been made the following year before the May changeover date and should be described as 1750/51.

Therefore an item being described as being made in 1749, (as E.J's initials were that year) could have been made in 1749/50.

This was the confirmation that Myra wanted to hear as she now had closure on the origin of this lovely old Silver Spoon. They both thanked Mr. Robertson who was tickled pink to be the bearer of such good news.

Myra believed that she now had the provenance surrounding the first distinguished owner, and perhaps now she could trace back Jamie Christie's connection.

PART TWO

— CHAPTER ONE —

The Honeymoon from Hell

After the events surrounding the deaths of their parents, life seemed to return to normal for a while for John and Myra. The Museum had a backlog of work for John, which kept him occupied and focused. At present he was waiting for his shipment from England to arrive with a virtual treasure trove of Antique Silver which had been found hidden in the Mayfair apartment. John was re-reading the manifesto to acquaint himself with the incredible collection which his Father had amassed over the years. Although she had a keen eye for quality, Myra was keen to learn more about Georgian Silver. James Robertson was very encouraging suggesting books on the subject and providing her with his expertise. They formed a mutual friendship as Myra considered him to be a man of character as well as a valued colleague for her husband.

'John we are really settled into married life but I would love to have some time away to celebrate our honeymoon. Is it possible to see some of this wonderful country?'

'I have been thinking along the same lines but I would just like to wait for a little while until the crates arrive safely. I have already informed the museum of my intention to take our honeymoon. It shouldn't be much longer before they arrive. In the meantime I hope it arrives soon because you are going to be up to your eyeballs in research into our honeymoon destination.'

His lips took on a wicked smile as he began to tease Myra about their forthcoming trip.

'I have been discussing it with the staff at the Museum. There have been some amazing suggestions so I hope you agree with what has been proposed.'

'Tell me where it is so that I can believe that at last we are really going.'

'You once suggested it yourself and I scoffed at the idea but now that I have heard quite a few differing opinions about the place it is looking good.'

'The only place that I ever mentioned in fun was Tim…..John you can't mean Timbuktu?'

'What do you know about Timbuktu ? I can assure you that it is a very old and interesting city which would guarantee a honeymoon which we would always remember.' Myra decided to do a little research herself. Having no idea what other attractions were to be found there she knew that a visit to the library would change all that. Armed with as many books as she could carry, she struggled home with her bundle of 'Information about Timbuktu' or 'Tombouctoo.' The opening pages were very disappointing as it seemed to be known as 'The City of Mud and Books.' She guessed that this place would hold a great attraction for John, but she was wasn't too sure about its appeal for her.

'Darling, please tell me why you have chosen this place? According to the map it is bordered by the Sahara Desert which means that it must be awfully hot and dry. I sort of hoped that we could explore some lovely waterways in this country like The Nile perhaps?'

'You are right about it being hot and dry most of the year but there are times when the climate is really quite bearable. The best way is to travel by boat on the beautiful Niger River which usually takes about three days, so we would be exploring lovely waterways. The Niger River is important because it carries only a tenth of as much sediment as the Nile but is relatively clear and pristine. The reason for this is because its headlands are located in ancient rocks which provide little silt. The Inner Niger Delta is a region of braided streams, marshes and lakes which are huge and teem with wildlife. This would be a journey to show some of the wonderful variety of the richness found in Africa, but the temperature is something else to consider, because it fluctuates between 13.6 to 42.6 degrees celsius.'

'Whoa, say that again. 13 to 42 degrees must be the most extreme fluctuation that exists on this planet. I don't know about you but my skin would turn to leather and my hair to crispy string.'

John was highly amused at Myra's comments, but she was really made of strong stuff and he guessed that she was in need of a little persuasion.

'We can't go for a little while yet, so in the meantime I will consult the experts and find out the most comfortable time of the year for us. You can still read all about the history of this ancient city and let me know your thoughts about it eh?'

Myra pored over the books and indeed she did find many interesting details about Timbuktu. It was an important trading route early in the 12th century, with salt, gold, ivory and slaves as a part of its lure. It had known many conquerors. During its Golden Age it had scholars, with a University as well as a great centre of learning. She read aloud.

"Here there are a great store of doctors, judges, priests and other learned men that are bountifully maintained at the king's costs and charges. And hither are brought diverse manuscripts or written books out of Barbary which are sold for more money than any other merchandise. Timbuktu became a place where books were imported, written and copied. Astonishingly they still survive in private collections." As she read further Myra found this information quite fascinating. Her journalist's training had given her an enquiring mind and an intelligent appetite for the written word. Now she felt that there may be something of interest for them both.

The following day John informed her that the shipment was due to arrive soon, but in the meantime he wanted to discuss their proposed honeymoon destination.

'My personal choice for us to go would be the month of November which has a min of 18, a max of 37 and an average temp of 28 degrees. As we are in early September now, that would be in two months time which will come around quickly enough.'

Myra's enthusiasm waned a little when she heard about the climate of this city, but John seemed keen to read out aloud some facts from the library's books.

'There is so much history attached to Mali: "The golden age of Timbuktu flourished in the 15th and 16th centuries. The city itself had a pivotal position and it prospered as a trading centre with a fabulous wealth based largely on gold, salt, ivory, kola nuts and slaves. The mud buildings and narrow streets show no outward signs of wealth, but there are treasures hidden behind the massive bronze doors of the priests' houses. The cool and coloured floor tiles were surrounded by simple walls with sparkling jewels adorning tapestries that were fading with age. Many rooms were lined from floor to ceiling with books."

'That sounds very interesting but John we are not likely to see any evidence of those golden days are we?'

'Perhaps not my darling, but there is an old saying in Timbuktu: "Gold came from the south, the salt from the north and the Divine knowledge from Timbuktu." It is of interest to read that. "Goods coming from the Mediterranean shores were traded in Timbuktu for gold. Arab traders and black scholars were attracted to this city, where the camel met the canoe, but more importantly Timbuktu was at the cross roads where traded goods came from North and West Africa."

'I can see now that there is much of historical significance which deserves more attention than the limited interest that I have shown.'

'Don't worry my little pet, you will soon be able to make up for all that once we get there. In the meantime how about a hot drink of cocoa? I'm ready to turn in.'

The crates had duly arrived but there was one small hiccup. Of the six large crates sent, only five could be found. This was a crushing blow for despite the insurance which covered the value, John felt a savage loss of these beautiful objects. He was told that all enquiries would be made in London from the shipping port together with the transport company which took the responsibility of shipping them. That evening after relating the story to his wife, John examined his inventory to try to determine which pieces had been packed into which boxes. If he could at least identify the missing objects it would be a start. He found that they were mostly small pieces which included the collection of Flatware, whereas the other five crates contained large pieces that were more easily identified and possibly a little harder to shift if they were being sold.

'It seems so hard to accept but I feel that the inventory which numbered the boxes would have identified their contents quite easily to someone who had an illegal interest in them. Let's hope that somehow they will show up soon. Perhaps it has all been a terrible mistake and the crate is stranded somewhere. In the meantime I have been watching the assembly of those lovely glass cases at the Museum. Filling them will keep you busy for a while.'

The next morning at breakfast, John mentioned that she needed to have proper protection from certain illnesses which were not covered in her initial vaccination before she traveled to England.

'Your health card shows that you have been vaccinated against yellow fever, smallpox and cholera, but we also have to include Hepatitis B, diphtheria, tetanus, measles, mumps rubella and polio. Every African country recommends that you be vaccinated against Hepatitis A, Rabies and Typhoid, as well as Malaria in the form of anti-malaria prophylactics.' Before he finished reading them out, Myra burst out laughing.

'You have got to be kidding! All that will turn me into a pin-cushion and you expect me to go on a romantic honeymoon?'

'This is a serious consideration wherever we go in Africa. I now need to have my Revaccination for most of the same things so we both will have to get over it together. Time is on our side anyway.'

Myra mumbled. 'Me and my big mouth.'

After a few weeks of aftershock from the necessary injections the countdown for this great adventure began. John had not referred to his missing crate as he was still busy at the Museum arranging this wonderful exhibition of Georgian Silver. He insisted that all was covered by insurance before he left for this long overdue holiday. Myra learned more about Mali, the River Niger and Timbuktu. She was intrigued that a river could exist on the southern edge of the Sahara Desert. Not only did it exist but it baffled Europeans for many years because the river ran away from the sea into the Sahara Desert, then it took a sharp right turn near Timbuktu before heading southeast to the Gulf of Guinea. It is a boomerang shape. That was at least one familiar word for this ex-patriot Aussie. Myra read to John.

THE HONEYMOON FROM HELL

'It is believed that two ancient rivers joined together. (The upper Niger once emptied into a now-gone lake while the lower Niger started in hills near that lake and flowed south into the Gulf of Guinea). The Sahara dried up in 4000-1000 BC. But the two rivers altered their courses and hooked up. How amazing that we can read today the data of something which happened such a long time ago!'

John nodded in agreement.

'Forget all those movies which show you endless tracts of sand hills. Many people used to live on the edge of the desert thousands of years ago. It was a much wetter place than it is today because evidence has been found of river animals such as crocodiles on rock engravings in southeast Algeria. The landforms include sand dunes, sand fields, stone plateaus, gravel plains, dry valleys and salt flats. The highest peak in the Sahara is a shield volcano in northern Chad, so you can see the diversity of this massive land form. It is believed that the Sahara has a rock layer underneath it in places where an ancient river meandered to feed an oasis.'

'Oo-er, are we going to travel in the Sahara Desert?'

'No not as such. The Sahara covers large parts of Algeria, Chad, Egypt, Libya, Mali, Mauritania, Morocco, Niger, Western Sahara, Sudan and Tunisia. We will just be visiting a small part of Mali and although it will be hot and dry, it will be fascinating.'

Myra smiled at his enthusiasm which had not been too evident just lately. She tried to show the same interest.

'I have read so much about the mud houses, but what sort of accommodation will we expect? Will we be staying in a hotel or perhaps a bed and breakfast establishment?'

'Neither my dear. I have managed to book us into an Inn.'

'An Inn? That sounds very much like the biblical days in Jerusalem. Why would you do that John?'

'For a very good reason: Whilst we are there I want to meet some of the locals at a level where they will trust and welcome us. There is an unwritten law of hospitality to all strangers, but I want to explore this place thoroughly and for that I have arranged to meet a guide in an Inn and not a hotel. We are not typical tourists and should not be thought as such. You would also be intrigued with the many tribes and races that have worked, traded and lived here. Have you come across Emperor Moussa or the Queen of Sheba yet amongst your reading material?' Myra was incredulous.

'The Queen of Sheba? I thought that she was just a legend!'

'Perhaps she was but some believe that she existed. King Solomon did!'

'I had better get back to my research. This is becoming really intriguing and perhaps more than interesting. I can see that there is so much that I have to learn about Mali and Timbuktu.'

'There is much to consider. It will be ongoing when we are there, but in the interim it will help if we can study their culture, and prepare ourselves for a very different part of Africa. What we also have to discuss is our method of travel. We have a few options: by truck, ferry, chartered boat or van. I would imagine that the most pleasant way would be by boat on the Niger River, as the red dust and sand have a nasty habit of getting into everything that comes near it. It should be less stressful and more picturesque as the river will pass some small fishing villages and the wild life is obviously more abundant.'

'Sounds good to me. I will leave this in your hands whilst I try to discover more about King Solomon and the Queen of Sheba.'

Over a course of the next few weeks, Myra became immersed in the history of Timbuktu and its Golden Age. This incredible image of a lost city of gold was balanced by the figures purported to be close to one third of the population being enslaved. She told John about her research.

"Many slaves preferred a life of slavery to 'economically precarious freedom.' It was believed that household slaves were better off than those who laboured in the salt mines. Apart from slaves, ivory, gold and salt, the legend of Timbuktu during the fourteenth century tells of a rich cultural centre of learning. In 1324 the Emperor of Mali, Mansa Moussa made his pilgrimage to Mecca via Cairo. He was accompanied by an entourage of 60,000 people and 200 camels, all laden with food, clothing and by one account more than two tons of gold. When he stopped in Egypt, the Egyptian currency lost its value and took several years to recover."

She stopped reading.

'Wow,' exclaimed Myra.' This is really amazing and unbelievable stuff. We never learned about any of this at school. I can see how you must find the everyday world so 'ho-hum' in comparison.'

John winked at her.

'Not with you in it now, my darling.'

Myra continued.

'Timbuktu was founded by the Tuaregs in the 11th century, but was ravaged by many different raiders as well as enriched by scholars and architects from Egypt and Arabia. A brisk and profitable trade in human souls for a thousand years saw the Tuareg sell and ship black Africans as slaves. It is estimated that 9 to 13 million black Africans were forced into slavery, many of them transported by the Tuareg. Although the Sahara divides Africa from the Middle East, the people who inhabit the Sahara itself, (the people of the desert) don't fit into either group. They are the nomadic Tuaregs who made Timbuktu one of the richest cities in the world before the city was lost seemingly forever. The Tuareg men belong to the world's only civilization where the men veil themselves, while the women go uncovered. Its purpose is to keep out the sand from the mouth during sandstorms, but also because they consider that the mouth is the most sensual part of a man's body and the most revealing."

'Well I never. Listen to this.'

"The mouth speaks truth or falsehoods, expresses fear and love can curse bitterly and yell insults, it can start wars. It can be slippery and sly and woo a woman with deceitful lies. It exposes the soul so it is better to keep such a powerful thing covered up."

She giggled to herself then continued reading.

'Still on the learning trail it also says that "Tuareg women are free and outspoken, but rather than distracting their men from their own carnal weaknesses by covering up themselves, they are the heads of the household. They are devoid of shyness will shake a man's hand and look him in the eyes. Although the Tuaregs have adopted Islam, it had been adapted to accommodate their unique relationship with women, and unlike Islam which permits a man to marry up to four wives, Tuareg women only allow their husbands to take a single wife. As circumstances dictate that the men are gone for long stretches of time which can be up to six months, the men accept the fact that the women who stay at home should take care of the family affairs. Ethnically the lords of the Sahara describe themselves as white, because they don't look Arab or black. Many Tuaregs have light skin, light eyes, sharp angular noses and cheekbones. Some legends say that they are descendants of an ancient Roman legion which was once lost in the desert." (Myra thought. 'How very interesting').

When John discussed their upcoming travel plans with his wife, he found a much more attentive and enthusiastic partner. Despite the fact that he told her that their destination was no longer 'The City of Gold,' but rather a city of mud buildings with its inhabitants suffering from impoverishment and desertification, Myra was enthralled by the accounts which she had read. John's main interest was in the manuscripts and libraries of Timbuktu, but he had read that so many of these priceless books had either been destroyed or moved to Marrakech in Morocco. Under French colonization in 1893 manuscripts were moved to French Museums and Universities. Myra was amazed at the revelations about the Tuaregs that had lived in this area for so long with their terrible involvement in the slave trade, but she listened to John's conversation about a subject which he knew well.

'Just as there are followers of Islam throughout Africa, there are also Jews who arrived from The Mediterranean, Egypt, the Arab peninsula, the Horn of Africa and Persia. This is borne out in notable archives containing records of an old Jewish community in Timbuktu. The Bantu tribes of Southern Africa still claim Jewish roots, as do groups in Senegal and of course Ethiopia, which is mentioned in the beginning of the Biblical Book of Genesis. The tribe of Judah includes the Ethiopian Jews who are descended from Menelik the son of King Solomon and the Queen of Sheba, who accompanied him from Jerusalem to Ethiopia.

I guess that what I am trying to say is this: Africa has been a melting pot of many races and religions. I am hoping that we will gain some insight into what is a fascinating history of this country.' Myra listened to these facts about her country of adoption and knew that John had a burning passion to investigate and explore this 'little known world' with its City of Mud and Books.

'When are we leaving?' she asked with a wide smile.

'I have booked our seats on South African Airways leaving in two days time. There will be a few connecting flights after Johannesburg, but from Niamey the capital of Niger we will have short car trip to Gao which is the river port on the Niger, and thence from boat to Timbuktu.' This all sounded well planned and concise, but it was anything but that. When they finally left South Africa, the journey was long, arduous with timetables which were at times unreliable or maybe even non-existent, but this was all part of the 'romance' of the journey according to

John. Even in this part of Africa the temperature could drop dramatically during the evening or the early morning. The relaxing boat trip was all that John had hoped for with magnificent sunsets which provided a magic backdrop to the start of their honeymoon.

Using her small diary, Myra sketched the diversity of birdlife and the interesting people along the riverbank. Once the boat had discharged its passengers in the early afternoon, John and Myra looked about them in amazement. They had stepped back in time into one of the poorest countries in the world. She took in the sand dunes which ringed the town in a glance and wondered how long it would be before the desert swallowed what was left. John wasted no time in finding their Inn, leaving her to unpack their belongings. He had the address of an English speaking guide which had been organized through the Museum. Walking down a narrow alley, he noted something which he hadn't counted on: sand and dust covered everything.

This home was a structure built of baked mud and stone with a Moorish style archway that led through a solid door into a courtyard. Its owner introduced himself as Mohammed and welcomed John in English.

'I am so pleased to meet you and I am happy to be able to help you in your quest to find and examine some of the wonderful old manuscripts which can be found here in this city.' John was more than satisfied that he had made contact. After explaining that both he and his wife were tired from the long journey, they arranged to meet at a mutually convenient time in the morning of the following day. As he returned to the Inn he reminded himself that this was their honeymoon and that he had better show a little more attention to his young and beautiful wife.

'Tomorrow I hope to possibly view some old manuscripts, but I have also found a local bazaar which sells some unique pieces of silver jewelry. It could be worth a visit for us both.'

Myra was just as keen as John to start their search for this fabled cache of ancient manuscripts and she was pleasantly surprised when their guide Mohammed was introduced. A tall man, immaculately dressed in white, who spoke perfect English, showed his evident passion as he spoke for a little while about their concerted effort to preserve and safeguard Africa's literary heritage. These words were manna from heaven as far as Myra was concerned. She listened with great interest as he spoke.

'Timbuktu was the Cambridge or Oxford of its day. Now we have a race against time to try to salvage and save what is possible to conserve. I will take you both to a storage room where you will find some wood and metal chests which contain some old books, but first I would like to give you some interesting information about the past glory of Timbuktu's history.

Hundreds of mathematical manuscripts, written in Arabic and various African languages from Timbuktu remain to be analysed to lift the veil from some of the mathematical connections between Africa south of the Sahara and the North of the continent. Only one manuscript written by al-Arwani (probably 16th century) has been partially analysed so far. What is also of great importance is the fact that many manuscripts survived this city's decline by being hidden in cellars or buried between the mosque's mud walls and safeguarded by their patrons. There are also some real challenges regarding the lack of humidity in this region because of the damages afflicted by it. Nevertheless we shall do our best as I am sure that you both will gain an insight into this wonderful heritage.'

John and Myra followed Mohammed for a little distance past a woman baking bread in an outdoor stone oven. The aroma was wonderful. Their guide assured them that they would have plenty of time to buy some later. He led them to another house and unlocked the door with an iron key. Inside a strong smell of mildew and stale earth accosted their senses. After adjusting their eyes to the semi-darkness John identified some chests which were covered in dust. Mohammed opened the lid to reveal some old books bound in mottled leather with covers which were decorated with grooved diamonds and polygons embellished with turquoise and red dye. Some were leafed in gold geometric designs with elegant Arabic calligraphy.

Myra was transfixed. As John picked up one of these beautiful volumes, the brittle leather began to break apart in his hands as pages centuries old, crumbled into scraps and fluttered to the floor. He stared in horror and disbelief.

'Oh, no,' cried Myra. She instinctively tried to try to pick up the pieces, knowing already that it was pointless. By now she noticed that the other books in this room were covered either with mould or bloated by moisture. How terrible for this to happen to John when they had just arrived.

'I am so sorry about this. I was only aware of their existence but not their condition. I will make sure that the next source will give us a better chance of success,' said Mohammed. John was bitterly disappointed knowing full well that this was not going to be easy. Adverse climate and environmental conditions were only part of the problem.

'Not to worry my friend, there is always tomorrow. In the meantime we are going to find some of that delicious bread and then go to the bazaar.'

Mohammed nodded and made his goodbyes. The marketplace proved to be a wonderful diversion. After sampling the freshly cooked bread with goat's cheese, the bazaar loomed as a welcome attraction. The weather was hot and dry with many uncovered wooden stalls set out in the open air. All around the sand and dust had settled, but the movement of the patrons' feet stirred it up only to shift and settle again. The noise was something else as animals competed with their owners to outdo each other. If the general colour of this place was dull, drab or overwhelmed by the sandy soil, it was more than compensated by the brilliant dresses and headgear of the women selling their painted woven fabrics and products. Myra was amazed at the lovely combinations presented for sale but she was more interested in the unusual designs of the silver jewelry.

'This is all so amazing that I wouldn't know where to start let alone understand what all these symbols and beads represent. I think that I may need some help from Mohammed. There are Silver and enamel beads, bracelets, pendants of all shapes with coloured stones, rings and some things that I don't recognise at all. I could do with a little explanation about the finer points before we purchase anything.'

'I agree. We could do with a little help. After the heat of the day has lessened we will visit Mohammed and see about this lovely Tuareg jewelry. Meanwhile I'm going to the library to do a little research on the manuscripts.'

When he entered their room John found his wife resting beneath the mosquito net which enveloped their bed like some exotic mushroom. Her little diary lay on the bedside table. She turned towards him with a smile.

'How did your trip to the library go?

'It was wonderful, but it opened my eyes to the poor condition of these manuscripts. Even though time is the real enemy, sadly so many have already left the country. Anyway I promised you a trip to the silver jewelry shop at the bazaar so let's go and see Mohammed. I feel sure that he would be an expert.'

'Okay, I have been busy too, writing my thoughts in this little diary and sketching things of interest so that I can recall them later.'

When Mohammed welcomed them to his home, he insisted that they sit and enjoy tea. This was quite an education as Myra watched this very different ceremony where the tea is poured from pot to small glass and back again a few times before it is drunk. It is black and sweet, and described by their host as the 'friends of conversation.' Myra liked that idea. John mentioned that his wife was keen to buy a few pieces of Tuareg Silver jewelry but had little understanding of it. Mohammed was more than happy to help.

'The Tuareg women have a superstitious fear of gold and will not wear it. Silver jewelry has both symbolic and real value which depicts the stories of a woman's city and her people. Some pendants include engraved maps of the palace of a sultan, whilst others are transferred from father to son at puberty. This jewelry plays many roles in the relations between generations and rites of passage, between men and women, courtship customs and marriage, as well as depicting wealth status and rank. You will find many different designs in fibulae which is a brooch or a clasp. There is a wonderful link to ancient and early designs that is a continuation of Roman forms. Not only were they beautiful but also practical in the use to fasten clothes and cloaks. Perhaps it is time for us to go and see what is on offer?'

He led the way through the dusty streets to the small stall where the jewelry was offered for sale, and began to speak in the local tongue to its owner. Myra was still in awe at the wonderful shapes and elaborate designs which were on display and picked up a few pieces to examine them more closely. One of these she showed to Mohammed and asked about it. It was a small ring that was topped with a square metal box and then a spire made from coloured enamel with beaten silver beading. The metal box was open on all sides and the base of the spire could be seen through it. Their guide took it from her and explained that these were 'hair pieces,' which were used to adorn and decorate a woman's hair. John was also interested in these beautiful examples of Tuareg craftsmanship and encouraged Myra to choose her favourite pieces. She chose a silver fibula with a lacy spade pattern and an antique bracelet with much intricate engraving on it, two pendants with antique Agadez Crosses, and two of the unusual hair pieces that reminded her of miniature lanterns. There were two silver bracelets that were very similar but Myra couldn't decide which one she preferred. One was smaller than the other which was a good idea as Myra thought that she would give one to her niece, Frances. As she held them and tried to decide, the seller became a little agitated and spoke to Mohammed in rather a harsh tone. John thought that perhaps they were taking too long, so he told Myra to take them both. This only seemed to annoy the woman even more, but after Mohammed had given John the price for these eight items she accepted the money with a muttered grumble and a stern frown. As they walked away Myra was a little puzzled and asked.

'What was that all about? Did I offend her by taking too long to decide?'

'Not at all,' said Mohammed. 'The two bracelets are the only ones that she has at the moment. She was hoping that you would only want one. The other fact is that these two are engraved with Holy Scriptures and she possibly may have thought that you would not understand or respect them because of your heritage. But please don't give it another thought. She will be happy with the sale because I added a little more for her trouble. Because these are not machine made products, a great pride is taken in the execution, and perhaps she expected a little more appreciation from us.'

'Thank you once again,' said John. 'We will turn in now and tomorrow I would like to discuss with you some of the interesting facts about the manuscripts that I learned from the library of al-Wangari.'

When the couple arrived back at the Inn they were greeted by Abu and his charming wife Debra who offered them a light meal of yoghurt and fruit which was quite delicious. After this Myra took her purchases to the small table and looked at them more closely. In particular the two antique bangles were fascinating. The smaller one fitted exactly into the larger one. When she placed one inside the other they seemed to line up into some design which looked like a pattern of rooftops in a city's skyline.

'How strange, look at this. These two bangles seem to be part of a plan or a map. When I place the little one inside the other, there are raised designs that seem to line up and follow each other.' John did as he was asked but couldn't quite make out what Myra was looking at, but promised to have a closer look tomorrow. The next day he was up early and eager to continue his quest with Mohammed.

'I have been informed by library staff and local historians that there are already 150,000 brittle manuscripts in Timbuktu, and it is believed that many more lie buried under the sand or in desert caves or underground chambers. This was done to protect them from Moroccan invaders, European explorers and then the French colonists. For centuries these remaining manuscripts have been a best kept secret, but now the race is on to rescue them before it is too late. My biggest worry is that collectors and duplicitous dealers could foil the attempt to keep them here.'

Mohammed was aware of the true concern shown by this man, believing that he had intelligence enough to understand the plight of the vulnerability of these treasures.

'There is much to consider regarding the preservation of these books, because as you know one of the most striking things about Timbuktu is the very low level of humidity. Unfortunately these extremely hot and dry conditions cause the paper to become very brittle and prone to mechanical damage. The paper is so lightweight or thin because there is so little moisture in it. This causes the damaged manuscript covers to impact on the pages which are turned back eventually snapping away, as you have already witnessed.'

'Yes Mohammed, I recall the water damage which we encountered when you first showed me those books in the boxes, but if this affects the ink and pigment as well, the staining will render them illegible. Then we have to combat termites which can turn a book into a three dimensional landscape that is also useless. I would like to think that there is a concerted effort to rethink and reassess the means of preservation.'

'I agree with you and I have been told that such practices will be considered. One idea is to separate the covers from their contents, and in this way the manuscript is protected by an archival card before it is returned to its cover. This will involve many hours, much patience and dedicated manpower. Unfortunately we do not have a great deal of any of these, so it is a very difficult task.'

'Sadly our time here is limited, and we have to leave at the end of next week but I will take this message back to Cape Town's Museum and try to find an answer. If I could speak or read Arabic or any of the African dialects from this area, I would offer my services, but you need scholars of repute and to rethink the understanding in a new dramatic way to show the origins of Africa.'

John knew that this tremendous work could take decades. He had received the message of the fragility and the ticking of time's clock, so he had to be content to admire the ones on show in the Library.

CHAPTER TWO

Myra Goes Missing

Africa 1953

With this sad realisation he returned to the Inn. Myra deserved a little sight-seeing of her choice before their flight home. As soon as he turned the door handle, he knew that something was very wrong. The room was in an uproar. Clothes and bedding were strewn around the room, the mosquito net was in tatters from where it had been ripped from the ceiling peg. Myra was nowhere to be seen. A window had been forced open leaving broken glass on the bed and the floor. He ran to the foyer and loudly rang the bell.

Immediately Debra arrived with a worried expression. This young couple had been so quiet that she hardly knew that they were there, but Mr. Collins looked very angry. She called her husband Abu who came hurrying in.

'Something has happened to my wife,' John told them. 'Our room has been trashed with our things broken and scattered about and Myra is missing.'

A loud gasp from Debra told him that she was really surprised, while Abu looked almost ashamed that this could happen at his Inn. The police who were called spoke enough English to get the facts. They asked John if any money or valuables had been taken. He told them that he always carried any cash in his money belt under his shirt. As for valuables they had brought nothing except what they wore: which was their watches and plain gold wedding bands.

It was too late to search tonight, but the police assured him that at first light tomorrow, their task would begin. John went back to tidy up the mess and also to pick up the pieces of glass. As he returned their clothing to the cupboard he noticed that some of Myra's silver jewelry purchases had been scattered around. He picked them up recalling that there were eight pieces in total. He could only count six. Picking up the bed linen and pillows from the floor, he felt something hard inside the pillow case. It was a silver bangle. Myra must have put it in there for safe-keeping. John left it there, deciding that he needed a good night's rest before the search for his missing wife continued. In the morning he decided to call on the only friend that he knew. Once again he felt a familiar sense of panic which had gripped him when Myra fell under a crowd of people in London.

Mohammed was horrified to hear about the kidnapping and was at a loss as to why this should happen. After he heard that Myra and one of her newly purchased bangles was missing he grew puzzled. Crime of this sort was very rare. There was really nowhere to hide a person in this area, or was there? He knew about the underground cellars, but this would be like looking for a needle in a haystack. There were also some caves on the outskirts of Timbuktu which could make a good hiding place, but who would want to take John's wife and why? He suggested to John that they find the woman who sold the silver jewelry and see what she had to say.

'I must admit that I didn't pay much attention to the things that were bought, except that the old woman wanted to sell only one and not both of the bangles. Even if your wife is wearing one of them now it doesn't explain why they broke in and took her.'

'This whole thing seems strange, but we have to start somewhere. Let's go to the marketplace,' replied John. There was no sign of the old woman. Mohammed couldn't find any details about her from the other shop-keepers. The police had no leads either. Enquiries would take time so Mohammed suggested that John come to take tea late in the afternoon. Because John knew very little of the language he was at a loss to search by himself. When he returned to the Inn he found Abu and his wife very concerned about Myra's disappearance. They both understood English so he told them about the fact that he had bought some silver jewelry from the bazaar before Myra disappeared. Abu was anxious to help and asked to see the pieces. When he saw the bangle Abu picked it up and examined it closely. Debra was called and they began to talk quickly in a language which was impossible for John to follow.

'Mr.Collins, this bangle is very old and perhaps could be an antique. As you can see it has much engraving that is not a continuous design, and the style of the uneven edges that project from the centre seem to be of an irregular pattern. I have not seen anything like this on sale before, so I can only guess that somehow it became mixed up with the other pieces and was not meant to be sold.'

'Thank you for shedding a little light on this, but for whatever reason this has happened, it means trouble.' Before John left with the bangle stowed in his money belt, Abu approached him with an idea.

'When all this took place my wife and I were in the kitchen and did not hear the window being broken. For this we are so sorry, but as it happened in broad daylight someone must have seen something outside your room. You are a guest under our roof. I feel that I must do my best to help you, so I am going to ask my brother Akmed for assistance. He is more than capable of making discreet enquiries about the disappearance of Mrs. Collins.'

John left with a heavy heart as he believed that perhaps they had made a bad choice in their purchases from the market. If they were valuable then that was reason enough for Myra to be kidnapped. When he met Mohammed, he recounted what Abu had said about the bangle which was still in his possession. After frowning a little Mohammed said.

'This is an unusual piece but I seem to recall that there were two the same, which seems to rule out the possibility of rarity. I am no expert but I can take you to someone who has expertise in this field. He lives a little distance on the edge of town so we can take donkeys as I am afraid that walking through the sand is not for me anymore. Besides it will be a new experience for you.'

Eventually they reached the home of Mohammed's friend Abdel, who ushered them into his spotless mud house. They were pointed to be seated on brilliantly patterned cushions on the floor whilst the tea was brewed. Mohammed explained to Abdel that John's wife had been taken in daylight from her accommodation and that a silver bangle was also missing. Their host was dressed in white flowing robes but he also wore a long blue turban around his head with a large piece that hung to the ground. John was struck by this man's brilliant blue eyes. After listening to Mohammed Abdel asked John to show him the bangle that was in his possession. He turned it over and around and then ran his fingers over the engravings without any comment before he handed it back to John. The tea was ready. John knew that this was a ritual which could not be hurried. Abdel poured from a height into small glasses and then tipped them back into the pot at least three times. After he was satisfied he handed them both a glass, then took one for himself. This was slowly drunk, more hot water was added to the pot and the same process began again. John really appreciated this custom as the donkey ride through the dust and sand had been thirsty work. After adding more sugar and hot water John drank a third glass silently admitting that this was a very civilized custom. Without any prompting Abdel spoke in excellent English to John.

'Welcome to my humble home Mr. Collins. My friend Mohammed has brought you here because he probably assumes that I am an expert in Tuareg silver. He is quite right but I am sorry to disappoint you because this is not an example. Although I belong to the Tuareg tribe I have chosen to live on the outskirts of town where I am not too affected by civilization. During my time as a silversmith I have seen all the many designs that are crafted by our people. This is not only our culture but also our history. We adorn and design our pieces with stories which relate to our past. Every piece contains symbols which illustrate that link. It is my opinion that this bangle does not contain any of the aforementioned details and therefore cannot be confused with the Tuareg traditions of Silver jewelry making.'

John was disappointed because the jewelry had been chosen with the belief that it was an authentic piece fashioned by a Tuareg craftsman.

He asked his host.

'If that is the case, is there anything that you can tell me about this bangle?'

'Yes indeed there is but before I do that I wish to speak to Mohammed about it, and if you will please excuse me I would prefer to speak more quickly in my own tongue.'

John nodded in agreement as he used the time to let his eyes wander around the room with its books, cupboards and objects which told of Abdel's culture and interests. The fabrics used on the cushions and rugs were exquisitely embroidered with beads in lovely patterns. He noticed a leather saddle sitting in the corner which was tooled and adorned with silver crosses. Obviously Abdel still rode a camel. Eventually after a few minutes Mohammed ended his conversation. Abdel resumed.

'I have just been informed by Mohammed of your sincere regard for the manuscripts of Timbuktu and also the fact that you are committed to help when and if possible in the future. This tells me a lot about your character and also your integrity. If you had just been a tourist passing through and expecting to use our treasures for your own ends, or even if you showed greed or disregard for them, my conversation would have been very different. What I am going to tell you will possibly explain why your wife has been taken together with the other bangle. This one is part of a pair. The other one would be smaller, with the same markings and extrusions, but it would fit exactly within the inner circle of the larger one. Is that correct?'

John nodded.

'There is a reason for this. It is not usual to find two together because they combine in essence to form a map. One piece is of no use without the other but I believe that they were both sold by mistake. What they were doing mixed up with the tourist jewelry for sale is anybody's guess. The fact that this one was not taken is a little puzzling, but perhaps your wife hid it? Finding her there was most likely a surprise to the men who took her.'

'What you are saying makes a lot of sense, but you still have not identified the origin of this thing,' said John.

'Ah, the origin. Well in my opinion this and its partner were fashioned in Ethiopia. The designs are distinctively Bedouin. Although not unlike the Tuareg patterns, these bangles have a heavier weight. More importantly the engravings do not relate to the symbols of our people. If it turns out that I am correct about it being a map I would advise extreme caution. It would not be wise to enquire about them from a museum or a library, because someone within earshot might overhear your questions. These two bangles are not attractive in a modern sense but they are extremely old and perhaps are desired by some unscrupulous people. I can make a few enquiries to see if any of my colleagues know the whereabouts of the shopkeeper from the market. It could be a lead.'

John rose with Mohammed and they both thanked their host for his hospitality. Arriving back at the Inn, John was greeted by Abu and his brother Akmed, who said hello in heavily accented English. He was a large man with a bald head, a black bushy beard which only accentuated his perfect white teeth. Abu had spoken to a few local men who regularly sat outside in the street, at first with no success. Later a young boy did give him some interesting information. The afternoon of the abduction two men with covered faces were seen at the back of the building breaking a window. They had grabbed the woman and pushed her out of the same window with her head covered.

As this all happened so fast they were away down the alley before anyone could cry out or try to stop them. John listened to this and tried to picture it in his mind. If these men had enough time to cover Myra's head as well as trash the room, perhaps they were not after the bangles. What else could they want?

Both Abu and Akmed promised John that they would help out in any way possible, once they knew where Myra was being kept. John thanked them both and went back to the room. As he lay on the bed he tried to recall what Myra had said over the last few days, when he remembered something. She had mentioned a small diary where she kept notes and sketches. Where was it? After looking through her clothes, the cupboards and her backpack, he assumed that perhaps it had been also taken. Retiring to bed early, he had plenty of questions but no answers. The next morning he went to the bathroom to shave. Reaching for his brush in the shaving mug, he found it seemed a little heavier than usual.

Myra had put the small bangle inside and covered it with water. The soap dish and razor lay alongside, but beneath the soap dish wrapped in a piece of tissue was Myra's diary. Myra must have thought about this, and guessed that it needed to be in a safe place. Good girl, she had used her intuition. Obviously the men who took her did not have time to search everywhere! He had his mind on other things when she told him about the two bangles fitting inside each other, so it had not seemed important at the time. He put down his razor and opened her little book. Flipping over to the last entries, he found what he wanted. Myra had made 'rubbings' of both bangles: each side of the larger one, as well as each side of the smaller one. Then there were another two 'rubbings,' when they were fitted together on each side. Six in total, but the thing which really interested him was that they each had a small internal catch. Myra had lined them up opposite each other and this placed all the engravings into some sort of order. She must have done this for her own curiosity realising that they would be safer if they were concealed separately. He put the bangle back into the shaving mug.

Mohammed was waiting for him after breakfast and told him that his friend Abdel was on his way.

'Good news, Mr. Collins. The men who took your wife were only amateurs who couldn't speak English very well. Because of this they were unable to explain to her what it was that they wanted.'

'Is she unharmed? That is of more importance to me.'

'Of course, I always seem to get around to the bottom line as you Westerners call it in my own time which seems to be circuitous to your culture.'

'Abdel, please understand that my wife means everything to me, and I will do anything to get her back.'

'Very well, I will continue with the other details because they have a bearing on the case too. The two men were given instructions to find the two bangles. They wouldn't have expected to come across your wife having a rest in the room. Kidnapping her was their only option because they couldn't talk to her or interrogate her. They decided that their employer would be able to determine the best method of finding what he was seeking when he spoke to your wife. Perhaps before or during the struggle, your wife managed to scatter the jewelry before she could hide it. Because she was an extra consideration which they had not expected, they panicked and left. Now to the details which you want to hear: This group is not violent nor is it dangerous. What they are seeking is the return of both antique bangles because these hold a very important religious significance. Their culture is such that they have been sworn to protect the secret that the bangles carry with them. (I have only hinted at it to you, but they are not aware of this).There will be no repercussions to the old woman from the market place because she became confused when the bangles were in a basket near her own goods and she picked them up thinking that they were part of her consignment. If you can assure me that you can place both of these into my hands, I give you my word that your wife will be returned unharmed by this time tomorrow.'

John knew that Mohammed had passed scrutiny from the Cape Town Museum. As he had introduced Abdel to him, he had to trust his word. There was really no other choice.

'Very well Abdel. Please wait here, I will go and get them for you.' He went to the bathroom, retrieved the wet bangle from his shaving mug then he removed the other one from the money belt around his waist. As he wiped the smaller one with a towel, he could not help but admire the beautiful and unusual pattern. Trust Myra, she had an eye for such things.

Abdel nodded his confirmation on the receipt of these objects. Somewhere within his flowing garments he found a small bag in which to contain them. This concluded their side of the business.

'Until tomorrow then,' said Abdel as he walked away. Mohammed saw the look of concern on John's face and turned to him.

'I am sure that all will be resolved. Abdel is a very powerful man who knows what factions would have an interest in Ethiopian antiques. If the police or other individuals had tried to interfere, the outcome might have been quite different. Apart from the religious fervour that is normal from this group they would not consider kindly any other unacceptable intrusion. Abdel is the one man who can do this.'

John understood that there were different ways to approach his problem and he had to trust that this was the right one. After saying goodbye to Mohammed a visit to the city centre to confirm their travel arrangements was something to occupy his mind. Once Myra was returned to him he knew she would be ready to go home. Walking along the dusty roads, he noticed how high the sand had crept up the side of some of the buildings, to where they became one with the baked mud used to construct them. The ravages of the sun together with the inherent fragility of the building materials were two enemies attacking this ancient city. Ostensibly he knew that it was a race against time which he could not stop, but he also knew that it was within his power to focus awareness on this ongoing disaster.

After confirming their exit plans by car, plane, and boat John decided to take a last look at the Museum. Because he had been a regular and notable visitor they had made him warmly welcome. For this reason he wanted to express his thanks for their kindness. Just as he turned to go, something caught his eye.

Whatever is that? It looks like a tiny silver spoon but it is so small that it seems impossible to expect that it could ever hold anything. He bent over and peered at it a little more closely then began to laugh. This brought the curator over to see the reason for his laughter. John explained.

'My wife has an insatiable interest in Silver Spoons and here in this cabinet is the smallest one that I have ever seen. Although I suspect that it is held as a pendant, I could never guess its purpose. Whatever is it used for?

'You have discovered something that is often a puzzle to some people but you are quite right about it being a pendant. This is an Ethiopian Silver Pendant "Ear Spoon."'

'An Ear Spoon? That is a completely new concept to me. Please tell me more about this.'

'Well, it was made in Ethiopia about the early 1900s and is made from a mixture of silver metal. It is small as you rightly remarked, and would be about 5 centimetres or 2 inches in length in your measurements. It was used to clean ears when needed, and is quite a useful implement when caught in a sandstorm. As you can see in this city, the dust and sand are always present. Even though this was fashioned in Ethiopia it made its way here because of a real necessity.'

'This is a piece of fascinating information about such a curious object. I will bring my wife here to see this before we return to Australia.'

True to his word Abdel returned Myra the next morning. He just nodded to John and left. There were no tears from her but it was evident that she was close to a state of mental exhaustion. He waited until they were inside their room before taking her into his arms. That is when she broke down and clung to her husband with an almost vice like grip. They both sat on the bed where he held her close as she told him the whole story in a shaking voice.

'I was kept in a cave somewhere near here but I was unable to see who was in charge. My two abductors had placed a piece of material over my head, which was replaced by a small cotton bag after I arrived at the cave. The cave was completely dark and stunk of the bats living there. When I was given water or some concoction of food my hands were tied. I was fed by someone whose face was also covered by a turban, so there is no way that I would ever be able to identify these men. I have no idea as to how long I spent there as I only fell asleep a couple of times on the low couch which was my bed. Apart from the man in charge who questioned me in passable English, the rest of the conversations were in a language unknown.'

'My darling Myra, don't distress yourself too much, I have you back unharmed and that is all that matters. Can you recall those conversations that were in English?'

'Of course. It was all about the two bangles which we had bought from the market bazaar. He wanted to know why we had bought both of them. I answered truthfully that I had bought one for myself and one for my sister's daughter who lived in Australia. He wasn't totally convinced but kept on about them. Did our guide suggest that we buy them? I denied that because I liked them immediately and had a good reason to buy them both. Our guide told me that he discussed the purchase with the seller, who thought that perhaps we were not worthy of such religious objects. When he gave her some extra money he assured her that we were of good character, both of which seemed to be accepted by her. My interrogator wanted to know if I had any idea about the designs or their origins. I truthfully answered that I had not. At all times he was courteous and polite and spoke in a quiet voice with a slight accent, but I did not feel threatened by him at all.

I had to lie when he asked me of their whereabouts because before the two men burst through our window, I knew that these were not ordinary bracelets and I took action that you would already know about. I had earlier taken rubbings, (as I had seen this done on the tombs of English Knights), which were recorded in my little diary hidden beneath the soap dish on the bathroom shelf. The details came up perfectly as you would have seen. I realised that the smaller bangle was of more importance than the larger one, so it had to be hidden too. Your shaving mug was the right size, but I covered the bangle with water and placed your brush inside it to prevent any rattling noise just in case anyone moved it. I hid the larger one in the pillow case. When the two men came through the window, they landed on the bed, pulling down the mosquito net and knocking me to the floor.

You know the rest. It was because they panicked in finding me here that they didn't bother to look any further.'

'My brave little one, you have been through an awful experience. If I had known that those two damned bracelets were so important to some religious group I would never have bought them. You are safe now. I'm not going to let you out of my sight until we board that boat in two days time.'

'I can only repeat that although I was at first frightened, I do not have any animosity towards these men. I can recall just how we both felt prior to returning the Coronation Anointing Spoon to the Tower of London. Some things are precious and sacred so that's why this could only have one outcome. I don't believe that they would have harmed me, but we had in our possession something which we were not meant to have.'

'You're probably right. As to whether they would have harmed you, I am not too sure about that. We were fortunate that my colleague Mohammed knew the best person here to affect your release. If we had not returned the two bangles it may have been a little different.'

Myra's head slowly dropped as exhaustion overtook her. Before her head hit the pillow he knew she was asleep. John partially undressed her, then he lay down beside her, gently stroking her neck and lovely auburn hair which really did need a wash.

In the morning she awoke, giving him that special smile that he knew so well. Knowing the importance of their reunion, they both celebrated their love for each other in the beautiful dawning of another day. Myra was first into the bathroom. She took a bath, washed her hair, checked that her diary was still in its place and then walked out naked into their room looking for some fresh clothes. John was with two minds as to whether he should try to coax her back to bed again, but today they both were going to pay a visit to the Museum before their upcoming departure. Myra made sure that she had her little diary with her as John had told her that there was something of interest which she may want to copy. At the Museum he led her to a cabinet with the pendant and its quaint little spoon. She looked, but had no idea what she was looking at until he told her that this was an 'Ear Spoon.'

'What the heck is an 'ear spoon,' she asked. John explained, but nearly had to put his hand over her mouth as Myra began to giggle.

'That is exactly what it is. So my dear one, what you see here is another silver spoon quite unlike any other.'

Myra nodded and when she was sure that they were alone, she took out her diary. Making a quick drawing of this quaint object took no time . She asked John to count the rows with the silver dots on them. There were also rows of engraving in the form of a twisted rope between the dots which were obviously hand crafted. After this was completed, she lingered for a little while at this cabinet because the objects were identified as being from Ethiopia. Despite her frightening ordeal, she was content. Myra knew that she had gained knowledge and an insight into the wonderful world of Africa with its variety of cultures. There was still so much to learn, admire and experience. That night they said their goodbyes to Abu and Debra, who were delighted to see Myra back safe and well. John thanked them for their kind offer of help and asked them to pass this onto Abu's brother.

Before they took the boat ride, both John and Myra wanted to thank Mohammed for his support and very real assistance. When John spoke about returning to assist with the manuscripts, Mohammed knew that this was spoken in truth.

'Our literary heritage is unique and wonderful. Timbuktu is crumbling in many ways, but it is in fact a lighthouse which lights up this country and the world if we can but keep it burning. Reading and books are the dialogue of time and space and our manuscripts may uncover some past secrets which will be of great benefit to the present and the future world. When you return I will be waiting. You know how to contact me when that time comes.

So for now, remember that "the gold came from the south, the salt from the north, and the Divine knowledge from Timbuktu". Farewell my friends. Go with God.'

In a short space of time they had seen and witnessed so much history, colour, culture and mystery. Even with the honest 'misappropriation' of a possible religious treasure, as well as the mind blowing visions of those ancient manuscripts, this experience was like no other. Myra knew the sincerity of concern shown by Abu and his wife Debra, as much as she felt the strength of character which emanated from Mohammed. Going back to a different world on the very same continent seemed to be a little incongruous, but this contrast only deepened their fascination for what other encounters life would provide for them.

Their plane returned them safely home, and before too long they were back into the usual routine of their everyday lives. As much as his work took up so much time, John couldn't help thinking about the incredible erosion of the manuscripts and the knowledge that was quickly disappearing because of the tremendous volume of these texts.

He waited until his Antique Silver display was completely stored safely in their new cabinets, and then decided to front his superiors about his concern. That night he talked with Myra about the unfortunate situation which was taking place in Timbuktu.

'Even if I had permission to go there in an official capacity, I cannot read or understand Arabic or the other African languages that are interspersed throughout these crumbling pages. It seems to me that we need a nationwide concerted effort to save this literary wealth. Just imagine being able to read texts that were written one thousand years ago.'

Although Myra was encouraging, she was only too aware that language was a real barrier when it came to translation of these ancient pages. In the meantime she wanted to discuss something with him about their time in Timbuktu.

'We never got around to talking about it, but where did all the gold come from which was taken by Emperor Moussa on a pilgrimage to Mecca via Cairo? Do you think that the gold came from this region or was it brought here and traded for slaves and salt?'

'That is really a loaded question. Maybe one day the manuscripts will shed a little light on that subject but until now it is inconclusive. Mali does produce a great deal of gold from a few mines which is proof in itself of the availability of the mineral wealth from this part of Africa.' Myra smiled.

'I suppose I am still dreaming about King Solomon and his fabled mines. I still have some books from our local library which have wonderful stories about the Queen of Sheba and her thirst for wisdom. After our brush with the religious zealots and your enlightenment on the lost pages of Africa's history, time doesn't seem to have much meaning in the modern day sense. Talking about mineral wealth, you forgot to enlighten me on the origin of the two silver bangles which we surrendered. I know that Mohammed helped you to arrange my release, but how did that happen?'

'When you were kidnapped, Mohammed took me to a man from the Tuareg tribe to identify the bangle which you had hidden in the pillowcase. I thought that it was Tuareg Silver because that is what we assumed when we found it at the bazaar. He discounted that and told us that he believed that it was made in Ethiopia. It was possibly a valuable antique, but he also knew that it was only one of a pair which could possibly be interlocked.'

Myra sighed.

'When I look at this map of Africa, Mali seems so far away from Ethiopia, but in truth, travel has always made trade possible.'

'You are right about that. The ancient caravans roamed from one side of Africa to the other as well as north and south, so it would be within the realms of possibility that this type of silver jewelry could have found its way here.'

The pile of books came and went as Myra kept busy learning about the ever changing population, climate and fortunes of Africa. In her opinion, Africa seemed to have the most changing religions, regimes and regions of any country that she had ever read about!

The missing crate had still not turned up and John seemed less interested in its whereabouts. He was working on an article about Timbuktu's need for recognition and he was about to read it to Myra. That was when she gave him the news.

'I am going to have a baby,' she said. John dropped his sheaf of papers. It took a little while for this to sink in, but when he saw her expression, he shouted.

'Wonderful! We are going to have our own little citizen of South Africa.' He stood up and went to hug her, but hesitated for a second.

'Come on, I'm not going to break if you hug me. It is still early days yet, so please don't announce this until I am at least three months gone. The Doctor will let me know when that date is confirmed. I guess that this conception took place in Timbuktu, so you could say that this baby was made in Mali.'

John laughed at her little joke, but he also knew that this would preclude any ideas about making a trip there for some time. This announcement was more important of course, but he had hopes that he might return there and help with the insurmountable problems associated with the multitude of manuscripts.

'You must take very good care of yourself my pet. The budget can spare a little extra to employ someone to help out with the household work when you feel it necessary. There will be so much that we have to plan. Apart from buying clothing and nappies we will need some nursery furniture. I am also thinking that it might be a good idea to buy a little bungalow of our own. We have the income from the rented flat in London together with my wage, which should allow us to purchase a dwelling suitable for my family. I will start enquiries for us to inspect some housing together.'

Myra was happy to see John so enthusiastic about the news, but she knew with the instincts of a close and loving wife that he had entertained hopes to get personally involved with the rescue of Timbuktu's treasures. When the subject next arose, she would encourage him to write articles from the Museum to the different heads of state, journalists and local politicians. He was good at this. The irreplaceable crumbling manuscripts of Timbuktu were an obvious part of his passionate obsession which she shared.

The next day, she phoned Jill, who was so happy to hear about the baby. She wanted to know all the details. When would the baby be born? She intended to start knitting right away, as every baby needed a layette. Where were they going to live? Did she have a good Doctor? Jill was happy to report some more good news.

'Mum's house has been sold. I expect the extra cash will be handy at a time like this. Brian will be sending a cheque with all the details very soon.'

'Thanks Jill, we are going to start looking for a house of our own now as this is only a small rented place. We can afford to buy something more suitable with that money. Give our love to Brian and the children. Bye.'

Both Myra and her husband were hoping to find a home before the end of the year. It would be wonderful to spend their first Christmas in the new house. There was not much time to do this, so John enlisted one of his staff to help with the search. He now had a shortlist of possibilities, so he phoned Myra to meet him and make the inspections. She wasn't keen about any of them but he understood her reservations as this was an important decision. It all came about by chance that Myra found her dream home. The regular visit to her Doctor found her telling him about the need for a larger place to accommodate her husband and their coming baby. He told her that he knew of a lovely house that was coming onto the market very soon. Its current owners wanted something smaller because their children had all left home. He would phone her in a few days and she could inspect it with her husband when convenient.

— CHAPTER THREE —

Home Sweet Home

Africa 1953

When this was arranged John drove her to the house set amongst a garden of lovely trees and bushes. The circular drive curved around to a front porch. Standing there was her Doctor and his wife. Myra was highly amused recalling the story about the couple wanting to relocate because their children had left home. After the introductions were made, the keys were handed over. The Doctor told them to let him know their decision after the weekend. The house was just what Myra wanted. She fell in love with it as she inspected it with a permanent smile on her face. On a single level, with a lovely garden and plenty of space for children to run around, it was more than suitable. Inside the rooms were spacious with high ceilings. Although it was full of charming furniture which probably would leave with the Doctor and his wife, everything was in an excellent condition. A price was agreed upon and the sale went ahead almost immediately.

Jill was true to her word: Brian's cheque had arrived in time to finalise the purchase. The Doctor's wife told Myra that they did not need the furniture as they were going to move into a much smaller modern home. If John and Myra could use it they would be prepared to sell it to them. (Myra told John that the price asked was so little that it would have cost more to get a furniture removalist to take it). They packed up their belongings and moved into their newly furnished home. John actually carried Myra over the threshold, because this was to be their new beginning. Their first born would grow up in this house. Myra decided to write a long letter to Ikey with their new address and give him all their news. She began with the fact that they would be parents in 1954.

The letter was also very descriptive about their honeymoon in Timbuktu, with its incredible manuscripts. Then there was the frightening kidnapping episode because of some religious jewelry which they had inadvertently purchased. Myra went on about the crates of Antique Silver which had eventually arrived, but she informed him that one crate was still missing. Lastly she jokingly told him that they didn't have time to search for King Solomon's mines, but perhaps some other time?

HOME SWEET HOME

A reply came back, so full of news that Myra laughed and cried with emotion. It made her remember all the adventures which she had with that motley group and how much she missed them.

Page two read this way.

'You both seem to be in clover now that a new mouth to feed is on its way. (Just don't use any of them silver spoons). Our good news is that Merv has married Flo next door. He looks like a real proper toff now as he serves out the coffee and cake. Me and me missus just loves our new place. She is the queen of our street and makes everyone aware of it. I must make a mental note to take her on another holiday! The antique shop attracts a whole new type of customer so we have had a wonderful reaction from the public. Those pieces of good stuff that you gave us really got us started off on the right foot. Now we have established a certain standard which has given us a good name for quality merchandise. The other great news is that Archie, who likes to be called 'Archibald,' has really come up in the world. Night school has done him a power of good, as his speech has improved out of sight. Sometimes he comes on a little strong, and I has to bring him down a peg or two. He dresses very differently now and plasters down his hair to look like Valentino, but there the resemblance ends.

If I'd known that you was looking for King Solomon's mines, I would have given you a letter of introduction. Be sure to keep in touch with your friends in the 'old dart.'

Ikey SOLOMON.

A.E. Stewart

This author began telling stories at the age of six in a Sydney boarding school. Once lights were out, tall tales were in. 'Ghost stories' were the most popular but it was the repetition of speaking and composing which produced words at a speed far quicker than anyone could write them down that started the treadmill. Such a place became the nursery where a vivid imagination was born.

A.E. lived in England for some time prior to the Queen's Coronation, where a wealth of experience with the 'Cockney' way of life and the different accents of the London population was gained.

The series of 'The Silver Thieves' was born from a younger brother's inspiration. His love of Silver and the borrowed 'Sterling Silver and their Hallmarks' book became the catalyst for this writer's literary intentions.

If you enjoyed this book, please leave a review on Amazon.

Contact A.E. ....jacana3@bigpond.com

The Queen's Coronation Spoon is stolen, leaving Myra to avert a national disaster.

Then in 1952 she comes into possession of a spoon stolen right from under the nose of Captain Cook himself, straight off the Endeavour in 1770.

Shrewd buyers circle, but a stubborn Myra obsessed with discovering the origin of Cook's spoon, hangs on through insurmountable challenges.

Excitement turns to disaster for Myra during the Queen's Coronation but the discovery of a cache of silver lifts her spirits; until religious fanatics ruin her honeymoon in Timbuktu.

A race against time to save the crumbling manuscripts of Timbuktu demand John's serious attention, but Myra's needs take priority as her life hangs in the balance.

The translation of the origin and the engraved message of the silver bracelets are revealed to John, but has he heard the whole story?

In the fourth century A.D. a young woman unites the nomadic Tuareg tribes of the Saharan Desert region.

Loved and known as the "Mother of us all," she is called Queen Tinan Hinan.

She commissions two silver bracelets, the engravings forming a map to the hiding place of a vast treasure.

But this connection to an ancient culture prevents anyone from unlocking the secret.

www.ingramcontent.com/pod-product-compliance
Lightning Source LLC
Chambersburg PA
CBHW020249150626
46552CB00020B/735